A Dark NA Romance erotica

by Best-selling Authors
D.H SIDEBOTTOM & KER DUKEY

DEDICATION

TO OUR KINKY KITTENS AND GROUP
SUPPORTERS.
YOU'RE TWISTED, DEPRAVED AND FREAKISHLY
DIRTY.

AND WE FUCKING LOVE YOU.
THIS ONE'S FOR YOU.

PROLOGUE

PROPOSAL

Star

THE SUN HEATED MY SKIN, its rays licking over me, branding me in its golden glow and warming my already sensitive body. The smell of lotion was intoxicating as the firm, familiar hands I craved rubbed over the contours of my body, rough fingers sliding along every inch of me. White sand and clear blue ocean as far as the eye could see relaxed me further.

This was what we needed. We both worked too hard, we never indulged or took time for just us two.

We lived out one of his fantasies last night; him taking me in the open where anyone could be watching, although making love under the blue hue of the moonlight on a secluded beach where he'd created a romantic bed of rose petals wasn't exactly where we could be caught. But it was still the most memorable night of my life, and hopefully his too.

I looked down at the twinkling diamond of my engagement ring and smiled. He had completely taken me off guard last night.

The memory played over, letting me relive the most magical proposal I could have asked for. Him pushing his body to join with mine before stilling when he was fully sheathed inside me. His soft gaze captured mine, his eyes glimmering with a thousand emotions before he murmured, "You were created to complete my soul, and mine yours. When the sun sets and rises every day from this day forward we will be forever entwined. I promise I'll give you everything. Friendship..." He peppered my face in kisses, his soft lips burying me in his love. "... Passion..." he thrust deeply, his hips pressing against mine, making me moan. "...Babies with my brains and your looks." He smiled cheekily, rubbing one hand over my stomach.

I gasped, slapping his shoulder which made him twitch deliciously inside me. I wanted to beg him to move; he filled me up completely but wasn't moving. His words made my heart thud and my mind race, their honesty drenching me in the truth of his promise.

"I'll support your dreams and live to make them come true." His eyes darkened, his gaze never leaving mine, hypnotizing me. "I'll fulfill every fantasy." His hand cupped my face, the softness of his palm both comforting and exciting. "I'll protect you, honor you, and God, love you more than anything."

My eyes were glassy; I couldn't stop the tears from forming. He continued as his voice dropped in tone, and his brow furrowed like he was concentrating, reminiscing. "I always felt connected to you, as if a string from my soul was tethered to yours."

His hand looped a thread around my ring finger. The tears spilled free when I noticed the other end was looped around his own finger, a platinum band with a huge diamond sat on the end. He tilted his hand, making the ring flow free down the thread until it encircled mine. I choked on a happy sob.

"Promise never to leave me, to never love another man. Promise to be my wife, promise to complete us?"

I couldn't speak. I wrapped my arms around him, bringing his head down to the crease of my neck as I nuzzled into his. My legs wrapped firmly around his waist as I dug the heels of my feet into his ass, urging and begging him to move.

His laugh resonated against my skin. "Is that a yes?" His head lifted to look into my eyes.

I swallowed and inhaled, catching the breath I needed. "I can't

2

promise I will never love another man," I whispered against his ear. His body stilled. I quickly continued before I ruined the moment and he passed out from lack of oxygen. "If he looks like you." His eyes widened. "And calls me Mommy, I will love him."

His breath rushed out of him, warming my lips. "Promise me!" he demanded with a thrust of his hips. His full length glided against my inner walls, eliciting pleasure into my core. "Promise me," he growled in frustration as his body covered every part of mine.

"I promise, I promise!" I cried out as he took me over the edge, onwards to make a start on the promises we both made.

CHAPTER 1

AWAKEN

Star

MY TONGUE WAS STUCK TO the roof of my mouth. *So dry.* I needed water. Everything was dry; my mouth, my eyes, even my joints felt brittle and tight.

My mind tackled the hazy fog, attempting to clear a path into consciousness. My body raged war with my mind, wanting to keep me in the sanctuary of my dreams, but my body needed hydrating, urging me to waken.

My eyelids felt heavy, too heavy, weighted down. What was wrong with me?

Peeling them open, darkness held my vision captive, the blackness creating frightening shadows of uncertainty. The only sound around me was my own heavy breaths.

I searched my memory for... well, *ANYTHING*! There was nothing there. Panic rose in my chest, my heart rate picking up pace, threatening to send me into cardiac arrest.

I jolted upright, groaning when a fierce pain exploded behind my eyes.

"Argh!" My hands cradled my head, the intense heavy throb too demanding for my shoulders.

I tried again, grasping for scraps. Who was I? Where was I? What was my name? Hell I didn't even know how old I was. Fear coursed through me, sending me scuttling backwards into a wall. The cold concrete crept through my spine and into my skin, lacing me in goose bumps from the chill and terror racing through my veins.

I was on a bed; I felt the softness of a mattress beneath me. I tried to swallow but there was no saliva in my mouth, my teeth sticking to my lips as I ran my tongue around them, desperately trying to apply some moisture.

A hum resonated before a blinking light flashed in the room, exposing more shadows that stole my breath. Unknown shapes and silhouettes startled me, shifting the dread in my heart up my throat. Darkness flashed again before light flooded in, burning my eyes from the harsh exposure after having not even a cast of moonlight.

It was a concrete room with one wall mirrored. My own image looked back at me but it was foreign, a stranger staring at me; strands of dark silk shaped around an oval face, huge eyes wide as the reflection illustrated my confusion.

I slowly climbed from the bed, my bare feet making contact on the cold floor with a muffled slap. A chill ran through my body, feeding sensation into the numbness shrouding me and alerting me to the fact my bladder was full.

I ignored the steel door to my right, completely transfixed on the woman in the mirror. Tanned shapely legs were bare up to the thigh where a red lace dress covered an hour glass figure. It was extremely elegant, the red contrasting perfectly with the luscious ebony hair which flowed flawlessly beyond the waist. Eyes a dark blue sapphire ring encompassing a pale jade; intense and expressive. A petite nose and full lips that were slightly chapped, complimented with high cheek bones. She was stunning. *I* was stunning.

How could I know basic things like beauty and names of objects, yet my identity was completely absent in my mind?

I startled when the sound of the door unlocking echoed through the *cell*. I was in a form of a cell, that was the only word I could use to describe the room I was in.

The heavy door opened with a loud clanking. I stepped back, terrified of who would come in. A man entered; power coated the air around him. He was tall and wide. His eyes held mine as he strode towards me. I felt unsteady on my feet, fear causing me to stumble when I tried to quickly back away from the giant coming at me.

He had a bald head and a scar that sliced his face from his pale blue eye across his cheek, ending at his jaw. He wore slacks and a dress shirt, magnifying the sheer muscle of him as the material strained across his chest.

Reaching for me, he grasped my arms in his dominant grip. My body trembled.

"Who are you?" I choked out, my tongue feeling too big and too dry.

Clasping my hands together he pulled handcuffs from his pocket, snapping them closed around my wrists. "Why am I under arrest?"

Again, he didn't answer me as he raised my arms above me. Confused, I looked up to see a metal chain hanging from the ceiling with a huge hook attached. Realization of what he intended sent me into panic and I thrashed in his fierce hold. His grip tightened, maneuvering me with little effort. The height of the hook forced me on to my tiptoes with my arms pulled tightly above my head, stretching me.

Another man entered. He was smaller than the first, who had now stepped back next to the door, his hands clutched together on his lower stomach, his eyes looking straight ahead.

The smaller man wore a suit. He was taller than me, but not by much. Judging by his height I'd guess he was 5', 8". His blonde hair was gelled back giving me a clear view of his face which was young and pretty for a male. His blue eyes collided with mine briefly. I noticed I didn't feel fear like I had with the first man… maybe it was his feminine features easing me into a false sense of security.

"Don't panic. I'm not going to cut you unless you force me to by moving around too much."

What the hell did that mean?

He snapped open a small rectangular box and light bounced off a pair of silver scissors inside. I couldn't swallow the lump forming in my throat.

Tears exploded from my eyes in a torrent as fear crippled me. I wanted to lick at them to drag some moisture into my mouth. The salt from my tears felt like grit in my eyes, blurring my vision.

My instincts told me to fight to get loose, to do anything other than just hang there for him to do what he wanted, but my logical side knew I couldn't get free from the binds, and to struggle could risk him cutting me. Were they going to cut my hair off? Was this some form of military training or prison?

"Where am I? Please tell me," I begged. My thoughts ran rampant and tried to claw at things out of my reach.

The cold press of the scissors as they slipped across my shoulder made me gasp. *Snip!* Then the other shoulder. *Snip!* The weight of my dress gave way, exposing my strapless bra, the classy red silk covering my breasts alerting me to the fact I liked luxury, and that apparently expense was not something I worried about.

My eyes pinched closed while my brain roared scenarios too frightening to give credit to.

Snip, snip, snip. The lace fell from my body, a pool of deep red gathering at my feet. I stepped onto it to ease the frost of the floor against the soles of my feet. It didn't halt the cold air licking the rest of my exposed skin though.

"Exquisite," the man stated.

Snip. My bra fell as more tears slipped free, burning a fire down my cheeks. My nipples hardened against the change in temperature from being clothed to un-clothed. It felt like my body betrayed me when it was only a natural response.

I turned my head to look away from the first guy, grateful for my long hair acting as a barrier between us. I didn't want to see if he was looking at my naked form, hung like a piece of meat on display for them to do with as they pleased.

Snip, snip. My panties fell away. My heart plummeted as I was on display, completely vulnerable. The cool air whispered across my flesh, an icy chill surfing up my spine, coating me in dread.

He stepped away from me, appraising me. Gentle sobs shook my body and made me swing slightly, my toes struggling to reach the floor and steady the sway.

My heart nearly leapt from my chest when a shrill alarm resounded across the quiet room. The first guy pulled out a cell phone and handed it to the smaller guy.

"Yes, truly. Okay." He passed the cell back then leaned in close to me, the heat from his body encircling me. The material of his suit rubbed against my skin, making me cringe. His overpowering aftershave assaulted my nose and made my throat burn, once more begging for water. "Congratulations, he's pleased with his purchase."

At first I thought he meant the scrap of red lace I stood on, then realization hit me with force. My lungs seized and burned, craving air, but shock prevented me from inhaling. My mind worked cruelly against me, arguing with what was before my very eyes. What was this? Was I dreaming? Was it a nightmare, a lucid dream?

I sucked in a breath when the door slammed closed and the lights once more went out.

CHAPTER 2

DELIRIOUS

Star

FIRE, THAT'S WHAT IT WAS! It started off with a slow burn before raging into a full inferno with no signs of cooling. My shoulders were about to combust, the pull on them from holding the weight of my body was agonizing, my tendons hot and angry, yet my hands were frozen and painful.

I needed the bathroom. Holding my full bladder for so long had given me a stomach ache. My toes kept giving way to cramp, making the cuffs bite into the skin around my wrists, the already sore, chapped skin becoming raw.

"Argh," I cried out for the millionth time, my throat sore after my screams. My tears had dried but the sting from their path was still alight on my cheeks. I couldn't count the seconds as they passed, how long I had been left hanging there in the darkness. I didn't know but it felt like hours.

I was so tired, my heavy eyes wanted to close, wanted to escape into my dreams, but the pain kept me present, albeit lightheaded, and forever in a state of consciousness between the two worlds. My mind still kept my identity captive, thoughts now my only solitude as my memories were locked away tightly, access to them not only forbidden but impossible.

The lights flicked back on, making me squint against the intrusion. My pupils frantically tried to adjust. My heart thumped an unsteady beat against my ribcage, threatening at any moment to go out of control and drown me in panic and fear.

Food. The smell of fresh bread filtered into my nose, making my mouth water and invading my painful body, causing my stomach to growl in hunger.

The men from earlier became visible. The smaller one set a bowl of water on the floor, and a second bowl with fresh bread inside. The fact I was still completely naked made me fully aware of the bigger man who disappeared behind me. I tried to turn but his hot, heavy palm came down on my hip, solidifying me. His touch coiled my stomach, my skin desperately trying to shrink against his contact as I fought to keep the vomit back. I wanted to scream for him to remove his hand but he reached up and unhooked me.

My body immediately went limp, giving way to the pressure it had been under. He grasped me around the waist, keeping me from crashing to the floor. Lowering me down instead and bringing my hands into his, he unlocked the cuffs but refrained from looking at me.

A sigh left my lips as relief poured into me but it was short lived. Pain from the blood rushing back in made me want to scream and cry but my eyes were too sore to produce tears and these bastards didn't deserve any more.

Before I could stop him, he pulled my hands behind my back and re-cuffed them then pointed to the bowls. The son of a bitch. I wasn't a freaking dog. I wanted to kick out at him but I could hardly feel my feet.

Wanting to have more pride than to crawl across the harsh floor I looked up at the second guy, hoping he would have some human traits and take pity enough to pass me the water. The tilt of his lips told me he knew what I was thinking. "We are not here to serve you."

With that they left me with my hands bound behind my back, naked on the cold floor, too far away from the sustenance my body howled out for.

10

CHAPTER 3

PRIZE

Dante

SHE WAS STUNNING, EVEN IN a broken down state. Her body was what others could only dream of achieving, toned and curved to perfection. Her religious workout and diet kept her athletic body performance fit.

Her cries echoed throughout the room. She had been hanging there like a prize for over four hours after waking from a drug induced sleep that had kept her sedated for thirty-six hours. I knew she would be starving and desperate to use a bathroom. My little star was used to her luxuries but was also big into charity and had spent time in under-privileged countries; this cell was a five star hotel compared to some of the living quarters she had endured. Not that she could remember that life, and that made her mind mine to mold and play with.

Watching the horror and shock in her cat-like eyes through the mirrored wall keeping me from her but able to see everything made me smile. Malik locked her hands behind her back. Defeat shone clear in her features when Theo told her they weren't there to serve her. Her memories wouldn't let her remember that she did, in fact, have people to wait on her hand and foot.

The door clicked open behind me, alerting me to Theo's presence. I could smell his suffocating aftershave before seeing him. The heavy footfall that followed told me Malik had entered behind him.

"What do you think she will do?" Malik asked, coming to stand next to me as we looked at my prize biting her lip, gazing longingly at the water and food placed a meter away from her.

I took in a lungful of air then exhaled, studying her before replying with the only answer there was. "She will go to her basic instincts... survival."

Her body shuffled forward, her face pinching with a wince. The cold floor would be uncomfortable and scrape the soft velvet flesh of her ass. A tiny screech rushed from her chest when her body tumbled forward, her shoulder taking the brunt of the impact and saving her exquisite face.

"Is this necessary?"

I glowered at Malik. "Yes! Now shut up and leave. I don't pay you to have compassion. It's a weakness that won't serve you well."

He looked to the floor, refusing my stern gaze. "I just meant stage two will give you the same results, right?"

His questioning irritated me. He was the hired help, nothing more. If he hadn't been with me for over a decade and loyal to a fault, I wouldn't have tolerated his brazen questioning.

"She's ignoring the food," Theo said, dragging my temper back into the dark depths where it lived, waiting to get its hands on its true prey.

She had shuffled her body to the water bowl. Her soft red cheek tipped the bowl so some poured into her open mouth but most dampened her face and hair, trickling down to form a puddle beside her face on the floor. She growled in frustration, making my cock harden. I was an asshole for getting off on her in such a distraught state but I didn't hide my perversions. I liked to see a woman naked and bound, and this one was special, the pleasure greater than any I had experienced before, and this was just the beginning.

I watched her pull herself into a sitting position then get to her feet, her petite body shaking gently. She was impressive. She made her way to the bed and curled up into a ball. I nodded to Theo; within seconds the light went out and night vision cameras displayed her on the twenty monitors set up against the far wall behind me.

"Once she comes around to eating what's been offered, we'll move on to phase two."

Theo smiled up at me, the little bastard. It's amazing what people will do for money.

I ran my finger over my bottom lip as I watched her sleep. She'd taken advantage of the time we'd left her alone, and she was deep into a few hours' sleep. I couldn't move from the window, watching the soft lift and fall of her chest, her firm tits rising and falling provocatively, taunting me.

My dick hardened as I imagined my teeth biting down on her large dusky pink nipples, making her cry out as she fisted my hair in her fingers and demanded more from me. Because she would, I knew she would demand it before this chapter came to an end.

She stirred, turning onto her back. Her tits stood firm, showing off another of her perfect features as her hands remained clasped behind her back. I groaned and yanked out my cock, giving in to its command. Shivering with the first stroke, I squeezed my fist tight as I slid my grip over the swollen head.

Star frowned, her nightmares twisting her striking features into contorted fear. My sick mind saw only pleasure on her face, how she would look and cry out as I rammed into her tight, wet little cunt. My breathing sped up as I imagined her pinned between me and the wall, my cock slamming in and out of her as she screamed in both pain and pleasure. Her legs would wrap around my waist as she took more and more, until the pain turned into a frenzied want for climax. She would tear at my hair, bite my neck and scratch at my skin with her nails as I rammed into her one last time in a deep, hard final thrust.

Cum shot from my dick and I struggled to contain it in my hand quick enough. I groaned loudly as the echo of Star's scream filled my ears, her pleasure loud and ferocious.

I yanked a tissue from the box on my desk and cleaned myself up before screwing it up and tossing it into the waste basket.

I sighed and looked at my petite little captive. She needed to eat. I needed her to eat. She would need all the strength she could get. A grin grew on my face when I pictured what was to come. The pretty little princess with the fake smile wouldn't know what had hit her when it all started. But she'd asked for this. For a long time now, and I wasn't usually one for patience.

CHAPTER 4

MISERY

Star

I STARED AT THE SCUFF mark on the wall. I couldn't divert my gaze from it without pain taking my breath from my lungs. It seemed to aid me as it kept my concentration on something even through the dim light in the room, my mind deciphering images and creating tiny pictures from each grey mark.

Exhaustion had overtaken me hours ago and I'd slept, only to wake once again to the nightmare that had found me. I didn't have the energy to climb from the bed and attempt to eat or drink what they left me hours ago. For one my teeth were too sensitive, every nerve in my retracted gums screeching in agony as the cold air in the room tingled. And for two, food was the last thing on my mind. I didn't attempt the water, although I was so thirsty. I couldn't be bothered. I wanted to die, and I hoped that dehydration took me before the bastards who held me there did. Dramatic? Maybe, but my body lacked the basics to even function and the fear of what awaited me when the men returned morphed my thoughts into horror-filled scenarios, none ending well for me.

A click that sounded louder than it actually was alerted me to company before the eruption of light did. I didn't move. Although I had essentially given up, fear and dread still held my lungs tight as my muscles twitched in readiness.

I could smell a slight masculine aroma, not too strong but faintly heady and citrusy. I was mesmerized by how receptive my hearing was when each tiny breath of my companion filtered into my head, each inhalation sounding thunderous in the still silence of the room.

I frowned to myself when after a while, although the faint breathing still told me of his presence, nothing else did. He hadn't spoken, moved an inch or made any other sound.

Curiosity won over and I turned slowly. If I'd had the energy to widen my eyes then I would have. Something flashed in my mind but as quickly as it came, it disappeared. He was tall, his firm body covered in muscles that caused me to stare. His thick, dark hair was cut short but not harsh, a slight length to the top. But it was his eyes that caused my breath to exit in short little spurts. They were so familiar yet so foreign. A shiver glided up my spine, tricking my brain into a false sense of home. I blinked at him when an intense coldness reflected back from them.

"Hello, Star."

Star? I didn't reply. He continued to stare at me from his position across the room. He leaned back against the wall, his thick arms crossed over his chest, watching me with a slight tilt to his head.

"Is…" The words stuck in my dry throat when he quirked a brow at me. Fear trickled through my veins and my chest heaved as the use of my voice box triggered a tickle in my scratchy throat, causing me to cough and splutter. He didn't assist me, just watched as I coughed and hacked at the dryness.

"Maybe if you stopped being so stubborn and had a drink, then you wouldn't have that problem."

I frowned at him. He huffed and rolled his eyes as he pushed away from the wall. His slow walk across the room towards me saw me inching across the bed until the wall stopped me from moving any further. He leaned over me, grabbing hold of my wrists.

"Don't hurt me," I whimpered, although the pain from my raw wrists under his heated palms and the bite of the cuffs already hurt so much. I wanted to scream for him to release me and dip them in ice to cool the sting throbbing beneath the torn skin, matching the thud from my heart rampantly beating in my chest.

He shook his head and fiddled with my cuffs until they snapped open. He rubbed at my skin furiously as I sank further back from him, my eyes wide and frightened as I froze in fear.

He eventually moved back and held out a bottle of water. "Drink."

I blinked. I hadn't seen it in his hand before but then I realized it had probably been tucked under his arm. I lowered my gaze to the bottle and eyed it warily.

"It's only water."

Knowing but not caring that it was probably laced with poison, I snatched it from his hand and unscrewed the cap before taking long, greedy pulls of water.

"Sip it."

I lifted my eyes to him, still guzzling at the bottle ravenously. The cool water felt like honey coating my throat, appearing to have healing properties as it soothed the abrasion lining my esophagus and quenched the unbelievable dryness in my mouth; however when it reached my stomach it was made of liquid fire. Cramp and spasms immediately caused me to double over and clench at the pain searing through me.

The man sighed and shook his head. "Always were the defiant one."

I looked up at him when my belly eased its rebellion. "You… Do I know you?" My own voice sounded foreign to my ears but I swallowed back the loneliness it created inside.

He smirked but didn't answer. Watching him carefully, he winked then turned around. "Eat," he ordered before opening the door and slipping through, quietly pulling it closed behind him, the tell-tale click of the lock once more notifying me of my solitude.

What the hell had just happened? I was suddenly so angry. How dare they treat me like this? I didn't deserve this. Although I had no idea what I deserved or not, I knew in my soul that I wasn't a bad person. I couldn't actually remember being nice, or if I had been happy but I distinguished the goodness inside me. I knew wrong from right, even though I didn't have a clue what kind of personality I had.

The emptiness inside my head brought the furious release of tears until I sat hugging my knees on the bed, sobbing uncontrollably. I didn't know what to do. I had no idea of what would happen to me, never mind what… what anything. Damn it! It was all a jumbled heap of nothing in my head, a deep chasm filled with swirls that wanted me to grab onto them but I couldn't reach. Each memory was a spitting flash inside my mind that fizzled out when I thought I had grasped it.

"WHY ARE YOU DOING THIS?" I screamed as I launched the bottle across the room, and it bounced off the steel door, rolling across the floor and coming to a stop at the base of the bed. "CAN YOU HEAR ME? WHY ARE YOU DOING THIS?"

My throat squealed at the sudden violence after the period of inactivity but I didn't care, it was just another pain on top of all the other ones, all of them blending together until all I felt was one solid mass of agony. "LET ME OUT, GOD DAMN YOU! LET ME GO!!"

I shot up off the bed, my legs giving way. The fury racing through me gave me the strength to clamber back up and stumble towards the door. "LET ME OUT!"

I fisted the door, not caring that the steel was impenetrable or that bruising and grazes were breaking out over the paleness of the soft skin on my hands. I didn't care that my throat blazed with pain, or that snot streamed down my face with the torrent of my tears. I didn't care that my bladder gave up and emptied itself on the floor around me. I didn't care that my forehead hit the door with a heavy thud when I slid down it, collapsing on a heap on the floor.

All I cared about, all I wanted, was to get out. I wanted to go home, wherever home was. I wanted a mother's love, or the strong embrace of a lover, if I even had one. I wanted the security of knowing who the hell I was. I prayed to get through this alive. But most of all, I wanted to die because the unknown was a silent death of a soul. They had stripped me of everything; I felt violated beyond anything they could do to my body. They had raped my mind. How? Why? "WHY?" I choked, my voice box refusing me any sound so it was just a silent scream.

CHAPTER 5

LET THE GAMES BEGIN

Dante

EVEN IN HER CONDITION SHE still had a hint of cherry blossom scent from her lotion. Her now unruly hair still had a commercial shine one could only achieve from expensive products. She was still the most beautiful woman I had ever laid my eyes on and I hated it with so much fucking passion it fueled the anger simmering under the surface. I let the rage burn in my veins, fueling me for what was to come next.

"Malik," I barked into the phone. "Shower time."

I stood outside the door as Malik gathered Star from the ground, her naked trim body in the same position she had collapsed in after her bladder finally failed her. She had held out longer than I thought. His fist encompassed her upper arm as he half guided, half dragged her body. Her eyes didn't lift to look at me as she moved past me. She was defeated. The smile gracing my lips should have been bigger but I wanted more from her before I would let the power of victory settle inside me.

I followed them to the shower room I had installed especially for this retribution: A fifteen foot square room, tiled from floor to ceiling with a row of powerful jets against one wall offering hot water to rain down, the other end a hose attached to a cold tap offering an icy awakening.

I watched with mirth as her steps faltered. Her head rose to take in the other female in front of her, naked under the hot spray of the shower. I came up behind her, making her startle when I whispered in her ear, "This is Maria."

Malik released his hold, causing her to stagger. I grasped her in my grip, pulling her back against my front before continuing my taunt. "She drank her water and ate the food kindly given as a gift to her. She also held her bladder and didn't piss herself like a fucking rodent," I snarled, forcing her body away from mine with a shove. Her body gave out, stumbling forward, falling and colliding with the tiled wall.

Malik was already aiming the hose in her direction. I turned my gaze to him and gave him a firm nod. A screech retched from her lungs, the shrill echo ricocheting off the walls, before turning into shocked pants. The chilled mist coated my face as the ice torrent blasted over her naked form. She curled into herself as she tried to protect her body from the bitter assault. I relished in her broken stuttering voice begging for it to stop, her lips turning a deep mauve signalling the temperature of her shower matched the liquid ice in my heart.

"Enough!" I ordered. The shower and hose ceased, the only sound echoing in the room coming from Star's teeth violently knocking together, her soft whimpers muffled from the vibration of her shivers.

"Will you be more grateful, Star, and enjoy the gifts I grant you?" I mocked. Her eyes slashed to me, betraying her thoughts forming images of my death in her mind. My deep chuckle rang out into the room.

Theo appeared beside me with her bowl, the bread inside now stale and hard. I took it from him and placed it down in front of her, her body shaking with such intensity she looked like one of those hula dolls stupid fucks put on their dashboards. I watched the battle in her eyes as she stared down at the bread. Her jittering hand reached out and snatched at it. She huddled further into the wall, bringing the bread to her lips, her nibbling reminding me of a pet hamster called Ginger my parents had bought me as a child ; the little fur ball had fascinated me and switched on my curiosity with science.

Star's actions brought my attention back to her. Pain flashed across her eyes, making her brow furrow. Her hand wrap around her stomach which rebelled against the intrusion of sustenance after being starved. Eyes lowering, she continued to nibble at it regardless.

Twenty minutes later she finally finished. Her body tensed as she forced the final swallow down.

"Good girl, now take a shower." She solidified, her head swiveling to the hose abandoned on the floor. My answering grin had her body scooting away. "Calm down, Belle." I enunciated the words, letting her know it was a command more than a suggestion. "You will learn quickly that what I reward you with is a gift and should be accepted as such and appreciated. My leniency to ungrateful, stubborn bitches is minute."

I stepped forward, clasping my hands around her cold, damp arms and lifted her with little effort, bringing her body to mine. It betrayed her mind, seeking out the heat my body offered, pressing into me and making me hold back a groan. My body was also a traitorous bastard and wanted inside her more than it wanted to see her cry … Well maybe inside her while she cried.

"Go warm your skin under the shower, Belle. You feel like a corpse and necrophilia is not a fetish I favor."

My cock stiffened at her intake of breath, her head tipping up to find my face, jade irises being swallowed by her pupils. She diverted her gaze from mine as quickly as it found purchase. Tugging free from my hold and timidly taking steps to the shower it was then I noticed Maria was still in the room, as were Theo and Malik.

"Maria," I barked. Her eyes lowered, her head bowing towards the floor as she took tentative steps to stand at my side. I reached up to cup her face, rewarding her obedience with a smile. "Theo has a gift for you."

Her answering smile and whispered thank you was observed by Star. Theo handed Maria a small silk robe then left with Malik to wait outside. She slipped the smooth material over her mocha skin. She was a stunning woman but her beauty paled in comparison to Star's. The robe sashayed down her body covering her hard dark nipples, toned flat stomach, and bare pussy, stopping mid-thigh.

"Do you like your gift, Maria?"

Her large chocolate eyes latched on to mine. "I do. Can I show you how much?" She asked.

My eyes sought out Star, standing in all her naked glory staring at the interaction, her mouth slightly open. I placed my hand on Maria's shoulder, adding a small amount of pressure. She didn't need much encouragement, willingly lowering to her knees. Her hands greedily came up to my belt buckle then dipped into the now open fly of my slacks. Her warm hand grasped my stiffening cock, exposing me to her mouth with haste. Her full lips sucked me straight into her mouth until the tip hit the back of her throat making her gag, her throat closing around me.

"You see, Belle, Maria has been here a little longer than you and has learned her place. She welcomes the gifts I grant her, the affection she earns with respecting her superior." I held my face stoic as I spoke so as not to grin at her disgust.

I growled in her direction when I saw the shower was still off. "You prefer the cold hose as opposed to the hot shower I told you to take?"

Eyes widening, she spun and pushed the lever. A splutter then a waterfall of rain tap-danced over her flesh. She reached for the soap left by Maria and began to wash her body, every curve sculpted to send my senses into overdrive.

My hand gripped Maria's hair to hold her in place so I could fuck her filthy mouth. She was as experienced as they came, her hot, wicked tongue slurping at me like an ice cream on a hot summer's day. I was above average in size, my girth thick but she had no problem stretching her expert lips over me.

My eyes devoured Star, my thoughts raging war with reality, my cock plunging unforgiving into Maria's throat, imagining it being Star's slick, constricted cunt. Her lips were all pink and wet and tight, enticing me to flood her gluttonous inner walls with my cum.

Fuck! She watched me stare at the slit between her toned thighs as my brain told me I was fucking that and not Maria's mouth. Her thick hair slicked back, her natural beauty laced in beading water, her nipples pink and hard. Heat warmed my entire crotch, traveling up my cock in waves of pleasure, making it swell. A shiver rocked up my spine as the feeling of my cum actually being sucked, pulled from me, nearly brought me to my knees.

I drew myself free from Maria's mouth, hot spurts of creamy ribbon coating her face and dripping down her chin to her chest. My whole body tensed as my orgasm found its end. Lowering my eyes from the intense shock on Star's face, I gathered some of my cum on the pad of my thumb and swiped it across Maria's lips. "Rub me into your skin. You have earned to wear my scent for the night."

The scoff leaving Star's lips brought my attention back to her. I narrowed my eyes at her. "You too will seek the honor of pleasing me and wearing my essence on your skin, Belle. Now follow me back to your room."

Maria stood and followed my lead as I left the room, the soft tap, tap from their bare feet echoed down the hall. Opening the cell I had kept Star in, I gestured for them both to enter. Scanning the second bed now in the room, they both turned to me with expectant eyes. "You will learn to share."

I turned to leave, stopping when a question was fired at me. "Is Belle my name?"

I cringed on the inside at the weakness of my own desire and the truth slipping free and calling her Belle. She really was a beauty, the most beautiful girl in the room; in any room. Belle was an endearment she hadn't earned and didn't deserve.

"Your name is and will always be Star!" I ground out, not turning to look at her. She had already made me soften, giving her a fucking compliment by calling her Belle and coming from thoughts of her pussy while Maria worked her jaw. I needed to remember my reasons for doing this, allow the ache molded from betrayal and bitterness that was fused into my soul from an early age rule here. I couldn't let my cock, my eyes or the fire buried deep down in the pit of my fiber burn out the hate I had for her. I needed my vengeance... I fucking earned it.

CHAPTER 6

FRIEND OR FOE

Star

THE CHILL IN THE ROOM seeped into my bones, my body rattling with violent shivers as my teeth chattered. Drops from my wet hair trickled down my back and chest, causing another more intense shudder.

I reached behind me where I sat on the bed and pulled the blanket around me, holding it tight as I embraced myself. The abrasive material scratched at my sensitive skin but it provided much needed warmth and security.

I looked over at Maria who regarded me from the edge of her bed. She was beautiful, possibly Italian with the deep rich bronze color of her skin. Her long black wavy hair fell in wet ringlets around her shoulders while her chocolate, slightly Asian eyes watched me warily.

"Are you…?"

She tipped her head and narrowed her eyes. I couldn't get a feel of her. The way she looked at me so intently made me nervous but there didn't appear to be any animosity in her expression. "Am I what?"

"Are you being held here too?" I knew it was a stupid question but I wanted to talk to her. I'd been left too long without company; well without friendly company. My nerves were shot, blocking my mind of anything intelligent to say but I needed a connection, if only from a few words.

She gave me a small nod, her eyes fixed on mine.

I nodded in return. "How long have you been here?"

She appeared to ponder for a moment as she shuffled backwards on the bed and rested her back on the wall behind her, bringing up her knees so she could hug them. The silk robe she had been given slipped open, each section falling in a soft pile either side of her. I was glad she had her legs tucked up; otherwise I would have been treated to a view of something I would rather not have had. "Around three months."

My eyes widened as my mouth fell open. "What?" My heart beat frantically as my throat closed in. "I can't… I can't stay here that long!"

She shrugged casually. "It's not like you have a choice, princess."

I couldn't work out if she was making fun of me, or just using the endearment trivially. "But…" I swallowed back the sob and curled further into myself. I was so tired of crying. My eyes were sore, my throat was sore, my brain was sore. Even my lips had started to crack, the once soft flesh now blistered and tender. Exhaustion had settled in and taken the fight I had found earlier.

We fell into silence for a while before I started questioning her again. "Can I ask you something?" She nodded, her eyes once again finding my face. "I know this may sound like a weird question but do you know who you are?"

She frowned at me as though I was stupid. "Yes." It was spoken with incredulity, one of her eyebrows elevated high on her forehead. "Don't you?"

I shook my head briskly. "No. I… there's nothing in my head. The only memories I have are the ones I have created from being here. There's nothing at all before here. I don't know who I am. I don't know how old I am, or what I like for breakfast. I don't know what my favorite color is, or what I prefer to drink. I don't know who my girlfriends are. I don't know if I have a boyfriend. I don't even know what damn shoe size I am." Maria stared at me with wide eyes throughout my outburst, her eyes widening further which each of my revelations. "The only thing I know is that my name is Star, and… and I'm scared."

I looked around the room nervously when she didn't answer me. I had never felt so alone in my life, even though my life now only consisted of a few days. My heart ached as my soul reached out for some comfort. I chewed on my nails when the silence grew uncomfortable. "Why did you do that?" I blurted out. "Do that to... to *him?*" I added when she looked at me blankly.

"Suck his cock?" she asked, smirking when I blushed at her words. I nodded, too embarrassed to speak. She straightened her legs and leaned forward, resting her palms on the tops of her thighs. "Honey, you'll soon learn to do anything, as long as it makes life in here easier."

"But... *that?*"

She shrugged. "What's a blowjob if it grants you luxuries and his affection?" She sighed and smiled warmly at me. "Look, Hun. I don't have the words to make you feel any better about being here, but I speak from experience when I say I would rather be on his good side than his bad, and if that means pleasuring him sexually, then I will. But don't worry, he doesn't fuck you, he never actually fucks. It's just oral pleasure he seeks."

I nodded but her calmness shocked me. How could anyone allow themselves to do things like that, especially to a person they despised? Or maybe I had read her wrong, maybe she didn't despise him, maybe she felt something for him. I'd heard of captives falling for their kidnappers – Stockholm syndrome. Many different thoughts raced around my mind when I realized I could fall into that trap; end up feeling something for the man who disgusted every fiber of my being.

We both turned towards the door when it opened. The man who had blasted the icy water on me in the shower walked in. His eyes moved from me to Maria then back again. He placed two bottles of water on the floor, then a bowl containing what looked like soup, with steam curling from it. My stomach rumbled loudly when the delicious aroma made its way up my nose. I cringed when the man smirked at me, his thin pale lips pulling even narrower with his cruel smug smile. "Well, eat this time."

I didn't answer him, just watched as he walked over to Maria. He slid his palm over her cheek affectionately. She smiled up at him, her eyes wide and idolizing. "You're such a good girl." He held a piece of bread between his fingers in front of her. She smiled softer and then curled her fingers around his and took the bread.

"Thank you."

He nodded then turned to me. A scowl covered his face as his eyes roamed over the blanket covering my body. The disdain on his face caused me to lower my eyes, self-disgust transferring from him to me. "You either eat…" I jumped when he appeared before me with the bowl in his hands. "…or I'll shove the fucking stuff down your throat."

I nodded but kept my eyes fixed on my lap. He pushed the bowl closer and I reached out for it. He pulled it back, taunting me and laughing when I reached again and he took a step back. He bent forward and placed the bowl on the floor. I frowned, not understanding why he had told me to eat then moved the food out of my way.

"Eat!" I looked up at him. He scoffed and lifted a brow. "Eat!" he repeated slowly as though I was dense and couldn't understand him.

I shuffled across the bed and stretched my arm to pick it up. His foot kicked at my arm and I yelped, snatching it back to cradle the pain. "The bowl doesn't move."

I swallowed back the bile when I figured out what he wanted. My gaze flicked to Maria. She smiled faintly as she chewed on a piece of bread she had dipped into her own bowl and nodded encouragingly.

He huffed when I remained still and tapped at the bowl with his foot, reminding me, baiting me. I shuffled forward slowly and slid to the floor. My belly groaned again. I was so damn hungry, my stomach muscles twisted in pain with just the scent of food. My mouth watered as I crawled closer.

When I made it to the bowl I looked up at him for the spoon. He stared at me and shrugged. It was then I understood I wouldn't be getting a spoon, that if I wanted to eat, I would eat like a dog. My gaze drifted once more to Maria as she sat on her bed, dipping her spoon into the soup and bringing it hungrily to her mouth.

The soup had cooled when I ran my tongue across the top of the watery broth. I curled my tongue, desperately trying to create a makeshift spoon but it was so hard. The liquid was too watery and all I managed was to wet my tongue, yet I was so hungry, I carried on. I found if I lapped faster, I was able to get more into my mouth. The chunks were easier, my teeth clamping around each morsel so I could take it in and chew.

The man laughed as the broth trickled over my cheek, crusting immediately in my freshly washed hair. Hatred conflicted with the food in my stomach, bringing with it a need to vomit, but my heart told me to carry on, to feed myself.

I swallowed back the self-disgust, the humiliation and the misery and I ate. I ate to give me strength, I ate to fuel my revulsion and I ate to show them I wasn't done yet.

Maria watched me, her eyes on the rapid movement of my tongue. I couldn't work out if she was an ally yet, but I had the impression she would turn on me quickly if it granted her leverage and 'ranking'. She seemed nice enough but there was something about her that made me wary.

I knelt back once I had managed to get what I could from the bowl without having to squash my nose in the bottom. The man sneered at me, chuckling smugly as he looked from me to the bowl. "See how easy that was." He kicked the bowl at me, the remaining soup splattering over my thighs, making me flinch and scuttle back towards the bed. "Amazing what you can accomplish when you understand how this is gonna work."

I didn't answer him; I didn't think he expected me to. His mocking grin curdled the fresh contents in my stomach. He turned to Maria. "Prepare her."

My eyes widened. "What?" I turned to Maria, my eyes begging her for an explanation. "Prepare me for what?"

"Of course." She spoke quietly but serenely.

He left us to it as Maria stood and walked towards me.

"What are we doing?"

She smiled softly and nodded her head as if to encourage me. "We need to prepare you for him."

"Him?" What the hell? Who?

She sighed gently and held out her hand for me. "It's time for you to be *presented*."

Something told me, with the way she said the word and the way her eyes darkened, my presentation wasn't going to be something quite as simple as a posh dress to welcome the queen in. Nor would it be as pleasant.

CHAPTER 7

URGES

Star

I HADN'T A CLUE WHO I was being presented to but he had to have a perversion because I was dressed in tiny jeans shorts that rode up my ass, a tee that barely covered my boobs with the slogan *'Red Hot Chilli Peppers'* splashed across the front, the material just covering my ample chest. My hair had been braided into two side braids, and cowboy boots adorned my feet. I was completely free of make-up and feeling so sick to my stomach I could barely breathe.

"Ready?" Maria chirped as though she was dressing a daughter for her prom. Her over-eager smile showed too many teeth. I wanted to question her sanity, but who was I to question anyone I didn't have a functioning memory of?

The door clicked open and the big man who had showered me in ice water approached. His eyes flicked over my attire briefly before his giant-sized palm wrapped around my upper arm. His hold was light but firm; he didn't squeeze the flesh like the man in charge who tried to hypnotize me with his words and the intensity of his glare did.

I had no choice but to clumsily follow next to him. I could have been imagining the intake of breath he took as he leaned towards me, but I didn't, he was smelling me, which made my insides tense and stir even more.

I didn't understand the reasoning of my mind and body but when the man in charge did these things, he did frighten and repulse me but my body betrayed that and yearned for his touch. Yet this intrusion, the simple inhaling of my scent by this man had my body recoiling and my mind battering at my survival instincts to kick in and flee. This was the first time he had really shown me any attention apart from to give me orders and indifference which made him all the more frightening.

"Go inside," he mumbled gently, shooing me forward towards a slightly open door. I was wary, my soft footfalls small and cautious. I felt his heavy palm on the bottom of my back, coaxing me forward.

I lifted my hand and slowly pushed the heavy steel door open further. The shadow crept across the white tiled floor, revealing more of the room to my view. My breathing divulged the truth of my nerves but I tried to hide them behind my stoic face.

The pressure on my back from the giant's hand forced me to stumble into the room, its bright florescent light illuminating the space before me. There were three walls made from what looked like a mirrored glass, but maybe thicker. My eyes darted around, soaking in the scene laid out in front of me.

Dark penetrating eyes roamed over me as the man who confused all my senses sat at a large table set up in the center of the otherwise barren room. He was dressed in slacks and a blue shirt, his tie hanging loose like he had tugged on it at the end of a hard work day.

Heat burned bright in his eyes then simmered to anger, the furrowing of his brow confirming it as his eyes dragged over the length of me. "You've changed so much, but then not at all," he murmured. The air was still but also charged like the calm, thick atmosphere before a storm.

I shuffled from one foot to the other, unsure of what was expected of me. The room had my brain scratching for memories it couldn't reach. What was this place and why was I there?

I hated myself. I wanted to pound at my own skull and berate my absent mind for failing me so drastically. Thoughts were so jumbled I didn't know if I could even trust myself.

What he said earlier played back in my mind making my lips move without permission. "How do we know each other?"

His hard glare made me want to fade into the air, evaporate into particles and then be carried away through the vents to freedom. What was freedom for me? What if my world was worse outside? No, I couldn't believe that. There was something inside me, granted it was deeply buried under the fear and clogged thoughts but there was something that told me I wasn't alone. I had something…someone.

The scraping of the chair and heavy presence in front of me commanded my attention. An iron-fisted grip tightened on my arms. "Why would you think we knew each other?" he barked at me, the small spray of spit from his angry question misting my cheek.

"You know my name and said I look different but the same," I squeaked as he shook me. My head thumped angrily against the abuse.

He stilled, his eyes studying my face before he answered. "I don't buy stock picked from a cattle farm, Star." He looked down at himself then back to me with a quirked brow. Yes, he was beautiful and shouldn't have trouble finding any woman to cater to any type of need he craved. "I chose with reason."

I was surprised at how forthcoming he was being and decided to push for more. "So we do know each other?" My eyes rebelled against what I wanted them to do, making me want to poke them out with a rusty spoon when they focused on his lips as I waited for his reply. They were full, the bottom one slightly fuller than the top, pink and smooth unlike the chapped, peeling sore lips of my own.

The side of his mouth lifted into a smirk. I wanted to cry that he knew what I was thinking. "I know you! But you have no idea who I am."

My body deflated. If we didn't know each other then there were no binds that tied us to make him more human towards me. I was just a captive to a man clearly deranged.

A chill blew gently against my exposed skin. Goosebumps scattered over my still sore flesh, making a tingle shoot through my body. I jerked from the intensity of it.

A throaty chuckle resonated from his chest and I glanced at him in shock.

His head tilted like a cat's does when it's curious about an object. Dipping his hand into the pocket of his slacks, he pulled a small tin out and flicked the lid with his thumb. The smell of cherries lifted from the tin, teasing my nose. The pad of his thumb skimmed over the surface before he reached towards me and swiped it across my bottom lip. It was warm and soothing, a silky smooth layer of moistness coating my parched lips.

I gasped involuntarily from his gentle touch, my eyes holding his, trying to decipher his play. Was it wrong that my whole being ached from such a tender caress? I wanted to sob and be held onto and told that everything would be okay.

My mind raced with all the instability. I didn't have time to react when a warm palm slid up my cheek, cupping me behind the ear and bringing me forwards to crush me against the full lips I had been admiring not moments before. My body tilted into his and for a split second I allowed myself to enjoy the connection before reality morphed back in.

His scent invaded me. His warm comfort turned to the fire of the underworld, trying to corrupt me. His taste exploded on my tongue, mint and wine swirling in the wet massage as his tongue danced and explored every inch of my mouth.

Images reminded me of Maria's mouth wrapped around his cock. My teeth clamped down as anger and confusion drowned me in what was real. This wasn't comfort, this man had kidnapped me.

A metallic tinge hit my lips as a hand gripped my braids in one fist, dragging forcefully downwards. My head snapped backwards. My mouth opened, releasing the damaged tissue of his now swollen, bleeding lip. I stared at him and winced at the black orbs swallowing any other color, glassy and terrifying as he glared down at me.

"You kissed me back." He seemed stunned, his eyes wide and searching which made me feel even more like a needy, dirty whore. "You like to bite?" A shadow marred his features.

I tried to shake my head to tell him no but his grip was so tight I was frightened if I moved too much I would lose the hair that was confined in his grip.

"Biting, marking, drawing blood is claiming in my world, Belle," he breathed before pushing me forwards across the table. My stomach hit the surface, my face following. His hand pushed hard making my cheek ache on impact with the wood. The air rushed from my lungs. He was so strong, the weight of him impossible to shift. He was hard;

I felt his pleasure digging into my prone ass as the rest of him covered my back.

His lips rested at my ear, taunting me. "I like to bite too!"

Tears filled my eyes and leaked out. A weak, broken cry rippled through my compressed chest. The ripping of the barely there shirt had my heart exploding into a thousand tiny shards.

Oh, God, no! My body fought against him, flipping frantically beneath him. I heard him grunt and then I was moving as he yanked me up. I spun to face him, my hand coming up and round as my body did, hitting him across the face. Fire exploded across my palm from the contact and then my own cheek smarted, my body giving way under the power of his backhanded attack. I met the floor in a crumbled mess.

Anger fueled me, making me act foolish. I knew I couldn't win but how could I live with myself if I didn't try? I kicked my foot out at his shin, making him swear and rush me, grasping my attacking foot so it couldn't make a second blow.

I was dragged a few feet, the tiles making me glide on my jeans-covered ass. Before I could stop him he grasped my other foot. I wiggled to free myself but it was useless. He parted my legs, his smirk mocking me as he overpowered me. His leg lifted, pressure coming down on me from his foot. I shook my head, pleading with him. "You going to behave?" he asked, amusement coloring his tone.

I shook my head as I still fought to defy him, but said yes over and over. He dropped one ankle, leaned forward and ripped at the remaining strands of fabric left of my tee, leaving me completely topless. My nipples hardened from being met with cooler air. My hands instinctively cupped my breasts, hiding them from his amused gaze.

"Stand up," he commanded, releasing my other foot.

I knew he saw defeat in my eyes. I was too weak, I knew I was, but I was too scared of the repercussions if I didn't do what he asked. Maria told me he never wanted full on intercourse, so maybe if I didn't provoke him with violence which he seemed to enjoy, he would get on with whatever he planned and permit me go back to my room.

I maneuvered my forearm to cover both breasts while I freed my other hand to help lift my body from the cold floor. I looked him in the eye, grateful my tears had dried.

"Clean your mess."

My eyes pinched in confusion. I scanned the room but there was no mess, nothing out of place or dirty. I came back to rest on his face, shrugging in bewilderment but before I could ask what he wanted me to clean, his finger lifted to the blood still pooling from his fattened lip.

I sighed loudly, my beaten down spirit finally giving in. I stretched my free hand up towards his face but he grabbed my wrist, shaking his head. His other hand forced my arm to free my breasts, the bounce slightly drawing his attention to them. Heat sparked in his eyes like when I first arrived. "Use your tongue."

He was disgusting. I hated him.

I closed the few inches between us and swallowed the lump strangling my throat then swiped my tongue over his mouth. He added pressure, pushing the weeping wound harder against the soft warmth of my tongue. His eyes briefly closed. I coaxed myself to cover his lip with my mouth, applying a gentle suction. The tang from his blood burst across my taste buds making me wince. He groaned, which encouraged me to continue, adding more pressure and swipes of my tongue. The warm cotton of his shirt teased my nipples. I didn't want to feel anything but the anger; however, my body was a traitorous slut, making me despise myself more than I already did.

A gust of cool air hit my face when he pulled away from me abruptly. He guided my body towards one of the mirrored walls. "Hands up," he growled.

I placed my hands on the glass. It was thick and not as cold as I thought it would have been, like it was made of plastic rather than glass. His weight pushed me flat against the mirror. His hands roamed down my body, tucking into the jean shorts and tugging them down, tapping at my foot to lift so he could clear them from my body.

I squeezed my eyes closed as humiliation curled deep, but I didn't risk moving. I concentrated on breathing, in…out…in…out. Hot palms smothered my flesh. A yelp retched from my lungs as a sharp, piercing compression dug into the fleshy tissue, heat firing up my spine as the bastard bit me. A warm trickle flowed down my leg as an offering, blood for blood.

"She will always belong to me. The mind might forget but the body never forgets who truly owns it," he said.

He stood upright, his presence encompassing me. I turned my head to see him. He was so close. I soaked in the image of my blood coating his lips. He looked like a fucking vampire, the sick asshole.

Tears threatened to fall. I was sick too because the wet between my thighs exposed me to the fact that sometime between entering and then, I had gotten aroused from his twisted game. The lights flashed out, blanketing us in complete darkness until a dim light from the other side of the mirrors bled into the room, growing brighter and highlighting male silhouettes that were looking in.

I scampered backwards but was met by the solid frame of my captor. "You're such a dirty slut, Belle. Nothing changes with you."

My intake of breath was so sharp I choked on the rush of air hitting my lungs too quickly. "I hate you, you sick bastard."

His growl was haunting, drenching me in the nature of his reason for taking me. He hated women. He hated me, but like me, he was weak and betrayed by his body's needs and urges. His erection pushed into me from behind. His hand roughly cupped between my legs. I grasped at his wrist on instinct, trying to pull his hand away.

"You hate me, Belle, yet your pussy leaks your truth into my hand. You want me to fuck your tight little cunt, ease the throb you have there?"

"SCREW YOU!" I sobbed.

"Mmm, that wouldn't work for me. No-one SCREWS ME!" He emphasized the final words with authority and finality.

"I hope Maria bites your dick off," I snarled.

His other hand wrapped around my throat, squeezing to show me he could easily take my life. A small part of me longed for him to just do it. "Maria knows her place and you will too. When I shove my cock in that greedy mouth of yours, all you'll be thinking about is how far down your compressed…" He squeezed his fist tighter, making me frantically claw at his hand, digging my nails in, "…throat my thick cock can go. I want to fuck your slutty little mouth so forcibly you choke as my cum empties straight into your stomach!" His hold loosened, making me splutter. "Good way to get protein into you." He chuckled darkly.

My mouth hung open at his outlandish comment. "Who were those people?" My dry throat burned as I murmured my question.

He walked to the door and banged his fist against the steel panel. It clicked open. The giant filled the space. I covered my dignity the best

I could from his wandering eyes. I felt the trail like a stain on my skin even after he averted his gaze. "Take her to her room. Give her a robe to wear."

My eyes popped wide at his orders. Something so small shouldn't have been a luxury but I wanted to thank him. The little bit of joy from something so minor conflicted with my inner war. I didn't want to be grateful for something so trivial but I was. I wanted to cover my body and have some type of humanity and this small thing granted me that.

My lips moved with my feet. As I passed him I whispered, "Thank you."

CHAPTER 8

YOU HAVE TO HAVE LOVED TO TRULY KNOW HATE

Dante

HER SCENT WAS ALL AROUND me, tattooing the memories of her natural essence onto my brain. The warmth of her soft, naked skin that'd had every inch touched by me was an echoing recollection replaying over and over, making my palm tingle to feel it again.

I was acting weak to my needs in front of the men who had kick-started this plan in the beginning. It was always there, plotting and festering but they had forced my hand by underestimating me.

I hated how Jonson and Davies had the audacity to mock me … ME! My head rolled from shoulder to shoulder as I tried to calm the seething boil simmering in my veins. I had proven my power to them and yet this was just the start. I brushed down the front of my shirt then adjusted my still proud cock before going to them.

"Dante! She is truly a beauty," Jenkins said. I nodded in agreement.

"She really doesn't recall her memory?" Davies asked.

"Nothing of who she is."

"It's impressive, Dante but she was hardly begging you to fuck her like you promised." The smarmy little cunt smirked. I wanted to cut off his lips so I never had to see that cocky smirk again; however, showing anger is to show fault.

"It's been such little time and yet she kissed me back and obeyed my command after a little foreplay." I chuckled which was accompanied by all of theirs. I looked back at the room from which I put on the little show for them. "This is just the tip of what I have planned for her."

I felt the creep of his presence beside me. He was a sick twisted little worm who wanted authority and respect he hadn't earned and never would from me. He was born into money and perversion so he thought this gave him rights he didn't have. We were men of money and we indulged in frowned upon desires but that was the only common thing that bonded us.

I was self-made; my desires were all tethered around two things. Her and revenge.

CHAPTER 9

ONE'S BODY BETRAYS ONE'S MIND

Star

I STARED UP AT MARIA when she handed me a sandwich wrapped in Saran wrap. She nodded and smiled, encouraging me to take it from her. My eyes flicked to the small camera watching our every move. "It's okay. It's yours. Apparently he was pleased with your show to his friends."

I frowned but snatched the food from her, my loud rumbling stomach not allowing me to do anything else. "Thank you."

She shrugged and walked over to the small portable toilet in the corner of the room that had been brought in when Maria had. I diverted my gaze as she relieved herself, my cheeks blushing as the long trickle of urine into the bowl humiliated me more than it did her.

"Do you think we'll ever get out of here?" I asked her when she flushed and ran her hands under the tiny single tap beside the toilet.

She shrugged but didn't answer me. "So Star, tell me about yourself."

My eyes widened. We were hardly there to become friends and I still couldn't make out where she fit into all this. "Well see, that may be a problem since I can't even tell myself about me."

"You still don't remember?"

I shook my head, answering her with a gesture as I bit into the moist cheese sandwich. The filling was thin and rubbery but the way my stomach demolished it told me I was enjoying it more than I thought.

She smiled, almost secretly and I frowned at her. It was as though she was pleased I couldn't remember anything. "Well, let's guess."

"I'm sorry?"

She smiled wider at me and settled herself on her bed. "Do you feel... married?"

I stared at her, what the hell? "Uhh, sorry but how does one guess at something like that?"

"I dunno. Do you *feel* married?" she repeated, ignoring my bewilderment.

I sighed and searched deep inside. I pulled at my heart, asking it if it was full or empty. It felt stupid but she was right, something was there, something that felt like someone owned it, someone filled it. "Well, I'm not sure if I'm married but..."

"But?"

"But it feels like my heart is happy. Does that make sense?"

Her face darkened slightly as her eyes narrowed. However, she smiled and nodded. "Yes, that makes perfect sense."

I smiled at her, feeling lighter. Someone out there cared for me, made me happy. And through all the darkness that suffocated me, that little bit of knowledge made it almost more bearable in there.

"What's... your favorite color?"

I closed my eyes, blowing out a puff of air. I ran the colors through my mind and smiled. "Yellow."

Excitement bubbled through me. They were only small things but they were still parts of me I now knew. "And I like savory more than I like sweet."

Maria tilted her head in question. "Yeah?"

"Yes! I can tell from how my mouth waters when I think of certain foods. Oh my God, thank you..."

She stiffened, her face tightening when the door opened and the man who seemed to lead everyone else stormed in. "I'm sorry, Mr Troy. I didn't mean to..."

I stared at his angry face, his teeth sheathed behind his taut lips as I shuffled backwards on the bed until my back thudded against the wall. I couldn't understand why he was angry. But he was – very. She called him Mr Troy. How did she know his name?

"We were just talking," I said, worry for Maria causing me to be open and quite rude.

He nodded and smirked at me but then turned back to Maria. "Get out!"

She gawped at him, her head shaking from side to side. "I'm sorry. I'm sorry."

"GET OUT!"

She scrambled off the bed, her ankles twisting beneath her as she attempted to remove herself from the room as quickly as possible.

He turned to me, his stare hard and cold, his narrow eyes dark and haunting. "Care to indulge?"

I frowned. "I'm sorry? Indulge what?"

He stood still, watching me with a callous expression. "Get up!"

"Make your damn mind up," I spat out. Fuck him and his frequent demands.

I squealed, bringing my hands up to my head when he seized a section of my hair and yanked me upright. My face flung to the side when the back of his hand connected with my cheekbone. I fell sideways when he hit me again, my head banging on the side of the bed. "What the fuck is wrong with you?" I shouted as I wiped the blood from my lip.

"You think remembering will help you out of here?"

I shook my head. "No, I was… God, I don't know what I was doing but it was good to… to feel again."

"You need to feel, Belle? Huh?"

What the hell was his problem?

His fingers circled my throat, his grip tight but not choking. Lifting me upright, I gasped when my back slammed against the wall. He was an inch from me, his breath hot on my face. I shivered, my body locking up when he reached further and ran his tongue down the side of my face. Pushing his hips against me, his hard erection told me this scene was turning him on.

Everything was confusing. How could hitting a woman be a turn on? How could drawing blood from someone be an aphrodisiac?

41

"Who are you? Why are you doing this?" I whispered as fear rendered me frozen between him and the wall.

He slid the tip of his nose along my jaw, his deep inhalations causing a ripple effect through my body, a deep throb heating my lower belly. His teeth flanked my bottom lip, his eyes securing mine as he bit gently, stunning me as the effect triggered a reaction in my body I didn't like. "You feel me now, Star?"

I nodded, unable to form words as my body blazed in a heat I struggled to douse. Tears formed in my eyes as mortification ran deep.

His fists grabbed at my gown, pulling it open savagely. A whimper raced up my throat when he cupped my breast, his thumb causing my nipple to pebble when he slid across the taut flesh gently. "Oh," he breathed against my neck. "You feel that, don't you?"

"Stop it. Please," I pleaded as more tears spilled from me. "Oh, God, please don't do this."

His mouth descended lower as his hand slid up the front of my neck, his fingers splaying wide. He pushed me further back against the wall, bracing me under his hold as his tongue ran across the rise of my breast. His breath chilled the dampness his tongue left. His hold on my neck tightened as his lips sealed around my erect nipple.

I pushed against his shoulders, desperately trying to get him to stop before my mind followed my body's want, dangerously making me crave more of his touch. My heart clashed with my body which conflicted against the sensations running through me. It was like my body mocked my thoughts, dampness pooling between my thighs as my brain cried out in pain at what was happening. I wanted him to touch me but I hated that he was. I needed him to stimulate parts of me that shrank back from him.

"I own you, Star. Your body betrays you. It alerts me to your need for me."

I shook my head furiously but shivered again when his tongue flicked out and caught my nipple between his tongue and his teeth. His hold on my neck constricted my throat, making me lightheaded. But, that only added to the way I reacted to him. My arousal intensified as my brain started to shut down, allowing the sensations in my body to heighten.

"Your body never forgets."

My mind flashed, images shifting quickly, blurred pictures rapidly morphing into more distorted flashes. *"Your body will never forget."*

I gasped as the memory in my head disappeared as soon as it had materialized. His face had appeared with the memory. I'd never met him before, so how did I have memories of him? He was there, in my mind, and his touch had been gentle, his words a whispered promise.

The world shifted under me as I swayed sideways. Mr Troy, as I had heard Maria refer to him, slammed his hand on the wall beside me to stop me from falling. He seemed unaware of my panic as his hand swept down the front of me, his touch hot but very soft.

I clamped my legs together when he reached the apex of my thighs. "Please don't do this."

His eyes snapped up to mine. Fury rolled across the depths of his irises, turning his deep eyes darker. "You don't get that choice, Star."

He dug his fingers into my thigh, pinching the flesh tightly. Tears fell when he yanked my legs open. "Please."

"Stop with the pitiful sobs. We both know how much you love the touch of a man."

His teeth sank into the roundness of my stomach as his hand pushed further into me, his fingers meeting with the wetness of my arousal. I moaned my forbidden desire as a fire of lust scorched through my system, instinct driving my hips until his finger slid against my entrance.

He chuckled. "See. You need it, don't you?"

I shook my head, denying his words. "No."

"Ah, but feel how good it is when I do this."

I sucked air through my teeth when his finger finally slid inside me, the heel of his hand pressing against my swollen clit. "You're so wet already. Such a little slut. Always a dirty little slut."

I ground against him, begging him with my body to stop the debilitating need that drove me to insanity. Shots of pleasure rolled over me when he pressed the tip of his finger across the delicate part inside me. "Oh, God, please."

I hated myself for begging when my mind started to rebel over what my body craved. Mortification and humiliation brought tears, but so did the pressure building in every single part of me.

"That's it, Star. Take from me. You always take, don't you? Feed your selfishness."

43

His hand started pumping inside me as he inserted another finger, two fingers now pleasuring me. My clit throbbed as his hand rubbed furiously against me, encouraging my climax faster and harder.

Every muscle in my body clenched. I lowered my eyes to his as he watched me from his knees, the muscles in his arm contracting fever-ishly as he labored me higher and higher. A choked sound ripped up my throat as my heart beat too fast in my chest. Sweat trickled from me as my orgasm approached.

His eyes narrowed before he yanked his hand back and shot upright. My body screamed in need but I didn't have chance to sort through the emotion before his hands gripped my shoulders and he shoved me to my knees.

My eyes widened when he wrenched his zip down and pulled his cock out. He fisted it, his fingers wrapping around the long, thick length of him.

"Open your mouth."

I stared at him, confusion and shock rendering me stupid.

"Open – your – fucking – mouth!"

My jaw snapped open. He jerked himself harder and harder, his eyes locked securely on mine. His abs rippled and his chest heaved as his cum shot across the gap between us, the warm cream spraying across my cheek, my mouth.. His roar of satisfaction drove my own desire to a dangerous level as I watched the pleasure tighten his face. His mouth opened in awe as his head fell back and his hips jerked with every pump of his orgasm.

If I didn't hate him so much, I would have deemed him as some-thing of pure beauty. He was stunning in the moment of his ejaculation, his whole body hardening as his muscles confined him in a state of bliss.

His last shudder broke the spell and his eyes once more found mine. A cruel smirk played on his lips as he tucked himself back in his pants.

I remained immobile as shock took my inability to move and feel.

"You're welcome." He laughed when my eyes widened further.

He patted the side of my face and winked before he turned and opened the door. He looked over his shoulder at me, his expression dark and full of hatred once more. "Oh and if you touch yourself, then expect to be punished."

He said no more as he slid through the door and left me on my knees, my body throbbing in need, my mind full of self-disgust and my heart brimming with hatred at my own betrayal.

CHAPTER 10

SATISFACTION

Dante

MALIK STOOD LEANING AGAINST THE wall when I closed the door behind me. He quirked an eyebrow. "You're really enjoying this, aren't you?"

I smirked and patted his shoulder. "Jealous?"

He shrugged then pursed his lips. "You do know that I watched what happened in there?"

"I wouldn't expect anything less from you, Malik."

He nodded slowly. "Then you won't hold it against me when I tell you she's started remembering."

I slammed to a halt and turned to him. "What?"

He sucked in his lips and nodded more slowly. "You said something to her and it triggered a memory."

I cocked my head in question. "How do you know?"

"Because it was written all over her face. She looked at you puzzled after."

My stomach swirled as anger increased my heart rate. "It doesn't matter. It will be over before it is fully reinstated."

He sighed and eyed me warily. "Are you sure about that?"

I turned on him, grabbing his shirt in my fist as I shoved him back against the wall. "Don't ever question me, Mal. You and I go way back, but I won't tolerate your interference. Let me do this my way. She's mine. You understand? She's mine."

He held up his hands to soothe my temper. "I know, Dante. And I understand. I'm just warning you."

I glared at him, making sure he knew he had overstepped the mark before I dropped him and turned. "Tell Theo Maria is punished for her baiting. The stupid bitch could have ruined everything," I ordered without looking at him.

He sighed again but remained silent as he walked off in the other direction. I pinched the bridge of my nose, trying to push back the encroaching headache. It was too soon for her memory to return. I wasn't sure how much she knew. Was I safe if it did return?

A small smile played at my lips. Yeah. I was safe but far from done with her to reach my ultimate goal. I loved seeing my cum paint her face. She was a beauty but never looked more beautiful than when wearing me on her. She was pushing me. I let my anger and weaknesses control my motives in that moment. I could have taken her right then but anyone can be taken by force, there was no power in that. I wanted her to give herself to me willingly so she hated herself for it. Her pussy wanted me; she couldn't deny it when it clutched at my fingers, trying to keep me inside her body. I needed to leave her needing a release, leaving her hungering for it.

CHAPTER 11

CRAVING

Star

I SCRAPED THE INDENTATION INTO the wall with the spoon I was permitted to eat with now. Nine small marks, that was how many days it had been since Mr. Troy had been absent, only to me though, he would still send for Maria and as much as I should have been grateful, my heart hollowed a little more every time.

If I had displeased him and he was gaining affection from Maria, how much longer would he keep me around?

The looks the giant kept giving me made my nerves more frayed than the calm I thought he tried to convey. What if he was waiting for Mr. Troy to make a choice and then he got the leftovers? My heart began to stampede once again. My mind was my worst enemy in the confines of this cell. My mind was its own cell.

The time his fingers entered me kept replaying in my mind. Every time my eyes closed the scent from his cum was tangible. What an asshole he was, who does that and then says, "'You're welcome'? Like he was giving me a gift.

He was vulgar, forcing me to open my mouth, his flavor coating my lips and dropping onto my tongue. I hated him for having any effect on my body, but he had, and it left me aching for a release I refused to give myself, not just from fear of punishment but out of principle.

What kind of person was I that I would get off from my captive's abuse? A lonely one, that's who. I felt a deep longing inside myself for something out of my reach, not an echo of the memory to grasp, just the empty feeling in my heart. I could choke on the despair when it gripped hold of me. I found myself breaking into sobs randomly throughout the day. I was going out of my mind.

A tune kept humming from my lips but I wasn't aware if it was significant to me or just my mind trying to fill the boredom. I walked over to Maria's bed. She had been given a hair brush that she used to brush my hair out every night; a small piece of contact I looked forward to. When you are deprived of such simple things like conversation, touch, a small piece of anything is worth so much and I yearned to be comforted by it.

She had been gone for much longer this time. Breakfast, lunch and dinner had been brought in and she was still absent; it made me pace from my bed to hers. I inhaled sharply, stinging the back of my throat when the lights shut off. This was bedtime… was he keeping her for the night?

My stomach recoiled, an ache simmered in my jaw as I fought the sob trying to force my face to crumble. I was jealous. Damn them both. I shouldn't be jealous, I couldn't understand the emotion or where it had even come from. Loneliness made me need; a simple touch, a hard contact, anything so I could feel a connection with someone, anyone.

I tore off my gown, baring my naked body to the cameras I knew were in place around the room; I was counting on it. I would force his hand.

Lying back on the bed I dropped my knees, spreading my thighs. I buried the revulsion for myself deep under every other emotion I was feeling. Gliding a finger into my mouth to coat it in my saliva, I traced it down my body and slid it inside myself. My chest rose from the mattress, my hips lifting to meet my hand. Within seconds the light exploded into the room, making me squint from the intrusion.

The clanking from the door swinging open made me gulp. He was

standing there. I didn't understand the happy mixed with fear stream-
ing through my body at the vision of him there in a black tailored suit
sculpted to his frame, his dark green tie contrasting nicely against all
the black. His hair was ruffled from him running his hands through it …
or Maria's hands. I closed my eyes to quash my inner voice raging war
with my sense of what was right and wrong.

"You were warned, Belle."

My eyes sprang open from his deep voice glazing me in a weird
sense of familiarity. The giant appeared behind him. I hurried to cover
myself from his disappointed gaze. Fuck him, fuck them all. They were
playing with me, starving me of life.

Mr. Troy moved inside, allowing the giant to enter behind him, then
came over and placed a box on the bed. "Get dressed."

I opened the box; a deep red satin dress was inside. It felt beautiful
against my fingers. Lifting it out, a creamy pearl necklace caught my
eye as it lay underneath. I scooped it up, my fingers running delicately
through the few layers of stunning pearls. My eyes darted to Mr. Troy
who smirked. The giant had exited the room but he wasn't going anywhere.

I dropped the cover I had used to conceal myself and draped the
fabric over my head. The cool soft touch flowed over my skin, the luxury of the expensive material sliding elegantly against my body. A hiss
sounded from behind me. Ignoring him, I slipped the pearls over my
head, trying to work out how they were supposed to lay.

"They don't go there, Belle, although I'd be happy to give you one
that did." He lightly chuckled.

Confusion pinched my face, and he walked over to me. Taking them
from my neck he rearranged the loops then dropped to his knees in front
of me. His hand came out to tap my ankle. "Oh my God," I breathed.
They were underwear.

He caressed them up my legs, the beaded balls kneading the flesh
as they travelled up my thighs, skimming under the red satin dress that
had gathered around the top of my legs.

Cool beads came to rest over my bare pussy, a string of them sitting
against the crease of my ass like a G-String, two layers resting above
my hips. His warm fingers stroked at my flesh as they left me, making
the air around us thicken, his dark pools penetrating my inner whore. I

craved his touch and as much as I hated him for it, the craving was the stronger urge now.

He moved away from me, standing and turning to leave, crooking a finger over his shoulder at me to follow. Placing one foot in front of the other, I gasped as the pearls moved over me in delicate strokes. Biting down hard on my lips to stifle my heavy breaths, I followed his lead, passing the giant in the hall.

My footfalls tapped against the cold floor, and I stopped at a door when he did. It opened into a warm, richly decorated room; heavy curtains draping from the ceiling, creating a gothic vibe. The dark red matched the color of my dress. A dinner table was set in the center of the room.

"Sit."

Walking to one of the seats at the table I slowly lowered myself down. I jumped violently as he swiped his arm across the table, knocking everything that was on it to the floor. The cluttering noises made my heart stop, before rebooting with his next command. "On the table, Belle. You wanted to give me a show... I want it up close."

I didn't move. I didn't know if I could move. He refused to wait; he reached out, grasping a fistful of my loose hair. Each follicle blazed from his rough hands. He dropped into the chair at the other end and placed me between his splayed thighs. His hand relinquished its hold on my hair as he reaffirmed his authority with both hands digging into my hips, lifting and placing me on the table. "Like to taunt men, Belle? Like to touch your pussy and cum in my honor?"

My head was shaking back and forth. "I didn't cum. I couldn't for a pig like you," I spat. The backhand to my cheekbone stunned me, the pain exploding heat along my entire right side. Tears filled my eyes, my hair flailing with the sharp twist of my head.

The sound of the ripping fabric of my dress and my body jerking from his brutal assault now reinforced my attention on him. My pretty dress was being ripped straight up the center, his fingers tearing at the silky material. Why the hell did he bother to make me wear it?

"Let's test that theory shall we?" The shreds fell in two, some silk still on my arms and dropping to my sides, exposing my frame; naked apart from the pearls decorating me. His temper and lust were clear in his stiff posture, his glassy orbs burning through me; he was teetering on the edge and it was contagious.

He walked over to a cabinet placed next to a huge love seat then came back with what looked like a wand with a ball thing on the end. My eyes widened. Was he going to hit me with that?

"Lean back, place your hands on the table and hold yourself up on your elbows."

"What is that?" I asked.

His eyes went to the object then devoured my body with a look, making me swallow. "Feet on the table. Legs open."

I obeyed his command. The embers still burned on my cheek and I wouldn't risk another blow. Twisting the bottom of the wand-looking object he sat back down in the chair, giving him a full view straight between my spilt thighs. Lifting the object, he placed it on the pearls covering me.

OH GOD!

It was vibrating, making the tiny balls tap dance over me. It was taunting and incredible. I tried to control my thoughts, to think of something else but it was impossible, the tiny rumble of the pleasure beads coated my entire pussy with a delicious pulse. He added pressure right above my clit and my hips lifted from the table to reach for the building release.

"You're glistening, Belle, coating the pearls in your own sheen. Does that feel good?"

"No," I growled but my heavy breathing, hard pebbled nipples and writhing hips betrayed my words.

"Do you want to cum, Belle? Leak your release and let me lap it up? Want me to bury my tongue in that hot little cunt of yours? Do you want my big thick cock to fuck your tight little hole, fill you all up?"

Oh God. His filthy mouth was building me with the tempo of his movements. That magic fucking stick thing he was using made my insides tighten the deep pull in my core.

"Do you want it, Belle? Tell me, do you want me inside you, fucking that throb you have building. Does your greedy little pussy want to be fed? I can smell you. Damn, I want to fuck you. Do you want me to?"

"Yes!" I screamed, dying a little inside. My body was ready to combust. His chuckle mocked me.

His other hand gripped the top of the pearls resting over my hips and lowered them to my thighs as he stood over me. "You really asking, Star? Does your pussy want to strangle my thick cock?"

"Damn you, Troy, just fuck me!" I screamed at him. I was sick of the games. I just wanted to get on with the inevitable and release the burn inside me.

"You asked, Star." He dropped his fly, freeing his engorged cock. Instead of moving the pearls to the side, he used the slackened strings to cover over my entry and then without mercy, he forced his cock into the hilt, every inch of him coated in pearls.

I screamed out from the abrupt intrusion. I was snug all around him, my inner walls squeezing at him, the stroke of the balls felt unnatural in the most extraordinary way.

The smooth pearls were rough inside me, each swipe of them, along with his cock, stroking the pleasure higher and higher until all I could feel was our fucking.

There was no other sensation. No sound filtered into my head, no air filled my lungs; even my nerves had frozen, allowing only bliss to build with each plunge of him inside me.

He wasn't gentle, his harsh grip on my skin painful and cruel but my body ignited, my pussy clutching him tight so he couldn't escape from me.

I yelped when I was suddenly flipped over, the pleasure suddenly disappearing when he pulled out and squashed the front of my body into the cold table. A fire grazed my ass as his palm struck it, the slap loud enough to release me from my daze. I pushed back, demanding more, begging for more. I couldn't handle the incredible hunger inside me. I was thirsty for stimulation, panting for release.

"Look how beautifully your skin wears my mark, Star. My branding suits you."

I screamed again when he struck me once more, the blaze of pain firing up the scorch of lust. "Fuck me," I ordered through clenched teeth.

"Ask me nicely. Ladies should maintain their manners."

I growled at him over my shoulder. His spiteful smile poured hatred into every part of me, yet it still wasn't enough to dampen the need. I sneered at him. "Please fuck me, Mr. Troy."

He laughed loudly, his face full of beautiful ruthlessness that made my heart still. "I love it when you beg but let's not pretend you're a lady,

Star. We both know you're a dirty little slut and you proved it so easily it's disappointing."

He slammed back inside me, causing my back to arch painfully. My heart seemed to stop while it simultaneously sped up, the beat of it matching the rhythm of his fucking, the contradiction causing a severe pain to crush my breastbone.

His fingers slid up the center of my back, the palm of his hand pressing against every groove of my spine until he fisted my hair and pulled my head back. His balls spanked my clit with every thrust inside me, his fingers fired shots of pain through my skull, his thick cock stretched me to an agonizing fullness – and I freaking loved it. I relished in the pain. I savored the sweet bite to each of my nerves. I possessed the driving ecstasy that tore through me and used it to pull my orgasm from its depths inside me.

Pleasure rolled over me, my body vibrating in total rapture as he thrust harder and harder. The snatch of his hold on my hair increased when I felt his breath on the side of my face. "Tell me how much you love it, Star. How good my cock feels inside you. How your body is humming and begging for me to let you fly."

I nodded, screwing my eyes closed as my mind vomited with the betrayal of my body. "Yes," I choked out as the thrill became intoxicating.

"Tell me," he repeated sternly as he pressed a hand down between my shoulder blades, driving the pain to clash with the pleasure sailing through me.

"I love it," I screamed as my thighs started to clench. "Your cock feels so good."

He slammed inside me hard as his orgasm continued to rip through him. He yanked my head back further, the pull in my neck excruciating. "Open your eyes, whore."

The way he spat the words sent a chill through my body. I snapped them open as a climax so intense caused my body to seize, each muscle contracting in a blissful torture.

A sob tore from me as I witnessed them watching me through a glass window. Four of them stood, their hands pressed to the glass, their eyes heated and narrow as lust and depravity contorted their faces.

Yet still my climax hit, the stare from our voyeurs intensifying my orgasm until my bones seemed to crack under the pressure. I couldn't catch a breath as my eyes rolled and a delicious tightening in my body fired levels of pleasure so extreme through me that I felt everything sway and blur.

Mr. Troy jerked violently inside me, dragging me up to the surface of consciousness and then back down again when I felt the warmth of his cum flow inside me. I couldn't work out if it had triggered another orgasm or if it extended the one already locking me down, but the pleasure went on and on until my exhausted body sagged beneath the weight of him.

"I must say," he breathed in my ear as my body still shuddered beneath him. "That was a lot better than I thought it would have been. Whores usually have slack cunts. But you surprise me."

Nausea threatened as humiliation hung heavy in my heart. I had succumbed to him so easily. Given him a piece of me that I would never get back, nor did I want it back. It was tainted now; dirty and spoilt.

I remained still when he pulled out of me, yanked his zip back up and walked from the room silently. The lights dimmed then flashed back on. I stole a peek at the window but the observers had now disappeared and a mirror replaced the viewing pane. I knew they still watched me, still laughed at what I had just become for a man I hated with my whole being.

Swallowing heavily, I pushed myself up, ignoring the trickle of stickiness between my legs and slowly left the room, my soul still dripping off the table with each spilled pearl from the string that had severed with his brutality.

CHAPTER 12

CONTRADICTION

Dante

THE SMILE ON MY FACE contradicted the hatred in my stomach. I hadn't wanted to enjoy it as much as I had. My dick still throbbed in ecstasy, my balls tingling with the feel of release.

Her cunt was exquisite... as always, the way those tight muscles of hers molded round my cock like she was sculpted just for me had slammed home the memorable feeling. But it had been that moment of familiarity that had reminded me why I was inside her, fucking her, taking her in front of them to prove to them who I was.

Her begging me to fuck her had brought on numerous forbidden feelings, one of them too intense to categorize, so I had pushed that aside and concentrated on the need to humiliate her, to degrade her like she asked for.

Another smile tilted my lips when I opened the door to the room next door. Theo looked up at me from his chair and gave me a half smile.

"You get it?"

He nodded then touched a button, bringing one of the screens to life. I watched the images play over then reached down and hit rewind on one particular part.

'Please fuck me, Mr. Troy.'

I laughed, rewinding then replaying it. "Perfect."

'Please fuck me, Mr. Troy.'

'Please fuck me, Mr. Troy.'

'Please fuck me, Mr. Troy.'

CHAPTER 13

ANIMAL

Star

THE BEAT OF THE WATER felt good against my clammy skin, the steam from the shower clouding my thoughts further. My heart ached with the hatred that ran through me. I hated how I craved him, needed him. My body was constantly stimulated. I wanted to think it was because I hung on to the thought that it was just me craving attention, needing the connection that his body gave me in my loneliness, but I needed to be honest with myself.

I wanted him to make me feel good again.

I tipped my head back under the stream, rinsing away the suds from my hair. The river running down my spine brought on memories of Mr. Troy's fingers sliding down my back. I shivered, trying to remove the pictures that made goosebumps erupt all over my over sensitive body. The scent of the shampoo I found awaiting me today made the strands fall like silk. Everything felt sexual since the day he took me, my body sensitive to any slight movement or touch.

It had been three days since he had been inside me, or even visited me. I couldn't drive the thoughts away, the opinion that he had been disappointed in me. Had I not satisfied him like he did me? I didn't have any memories to compare it to. I didn't know if I had been good, or if anyone had ever told me I felt good around them. Should I care? *NO!* Did I? *YES.*

I asked to shower in the hope he would come to me. He had always been here in the past when I showered but today the giant had taken me to the door and gestured for me to go inside. I was alone.

My heart panged for something. I didn't acknowledge it was him; I put it down to my consciousness yearning for something from my past, something out of my reach. My memories were still keeping my life locked away in the darkness of my mind.

The turmoil inside me was incredible. I didn't know if this was my life, what I had been or was used to in my past. Was this normal for me? Was being here who I was? Yet deep down I knew the answers. This wasn't right. What was happening to me was far from right.

Maria had been brought back into the room the night Mr. Troy had taken me, surprising me. She had changed, however. Her abhorrence of me was physical. She didn't say anything or acknowledge our change of status, but I caught her glares, the ire in her stares. I'd caught her looming over me when I had woken in the night, the silhouette of her rigid, angry posture vibrating above me.

I didn't understand what I'd done but I couldn't help but think it was because Troy had taken me fully. Maria had said he didn't fuck, he just demanded oral pleasure. Was she jealous of me? Of the fact he'd gone one step further with me than he did with her? If so, that was stupid because it didn't make him want me anymore than her. He hadn't demanded me again and as much as I despised myself, it left an itch under my skin; a nervous humming. What if he was finished with me now? What would he do with me?

I cut off the shower and grabbed the towel from the hook then wrapped it around myself. A shiver crept up my spine. I took a deep breath, trying to bury the unease living in me before stepping out into the adjoining area. The soles of my wet feet slid when the guy I'd come to know as Theo stood leaning against one wall. His arms were crossed over his chest, his accusing eyes narrow, his cold glare on my face.

"I thought you were never coming out."

I stiffened as I pulled the towel tighter around me. I didn't like Theo; he was mean to me without cause making me wary of having my back to him or ever being alone with him - which had never happened until now. Oh God, why didn't I stay in my room and why did the giant have to give in to my request so easily?

"I'm sorry, the... my guard."

"Malik!" he spat. "His name is Malik and he's not your guard! You're not special enough to warrant one."

My eyes closed from his verbal whiplashing through the air, biting at my morale. "Malik said I could shower."

He shrugged and inhaled deeply. "I'm not arguing that. I'm wondering what you were doing in there."

I frowned, not understanding what he was getting at. "I'm sorry, I was showering."

He pushed off the wall, his short dumpy legs moving across the room until he stood before me. "Were you touching your filthy cunt?"

My eyes widened, my mouth dropping open at his crudeness. "What? Of course not." My voice trembled as fear shook me

He didn't reply. I stood stock still when his eyes dropped from my face to where my hand clutched the towel. Pulling it tighter, I shifted from one foot to the other. My eyes shot around the room. I didn't like how this felt, how the atmosphere told of his arousal or the way his eyes blazed hungrily with lust and distaste.

"Let go of the towel."

I gawped at him, shaking my head. "No… why…?"

His brows lifted, his jaw tightening with my refusal. I winced when his hand shot out, his fingers circling my throat, crushing my windpipe in his furious hold. "Don't tell me no, you fucking bitch."

A sob tore up my throat when he yanked at my towel, pulling it away from me and slinging it to one side of the room. Everything inside me seized up, nerves locking down my muscles, fear chilling my bones. I was used to my nudity being on display but not to be molested by this disgusting vermin.

My feet left the floor when he propelled me backwards, my back slamming into the wall, firing an agonizing pain up my spine as my head hit a shelf holding towels, bottles of shampoo and body washes. The back of my head cracked with so much force I felt a lump already forming. All the contents from the shelf fell to the floor around me.

I scrambled around, crawling along the floor to get away from him. His fingers circled my ankle, the sudden pull causing my face to smack the floor, in turn colliding my nose with the unforgiving wet slabs, making blood trickle down over my lips.

I kicked out at him, natural instinct fighting him the closer my body came to his. He was on top of me in seconds, his thighs locking me down as he straddled himself over my back.

"Come on, bring out the inner whore I know is in there. You love the fight don't you, Star? Love the thrill of it. You don't deny me because you don't want it, you deny me because it turns you on."

I shook my head rapidly. "No…. please…."

"I watched you. Watched the way you spread your easy legs for Dante. Watched you beg him to fill that hungry, nasty cunt of yours. God, you act too perfect but I knew there was a dirty slut in there."

His fingers yanked my hair, snapping my head back as he shuffled further down me, his knees parting my legs. I cried out when the whole of his hand cupped the back of my head and slammed it down on the floor. The world spun beneath me as vomit rolled up from my stomach, burning my throat on its mission to be freed.

"NO!" I screamed when his grubby fingers clawed between my legs, my gut rolling with his touch. "Please don't," I sobbed loudly.

"Fuck!" he hissed out when he rammed a finger inside me. "You're so tight."

That would be because I was so dry, but the asshole didn't notice that part. He was delusional, thinking my fighting was part of some sort of sick sex game.

"No wonder Dante likes to get off on you. Fucking tasty little slut."

I was scrambling around under him, my fingers digging into the tiles as I tried to get leverage to pull myself away from him. The sound of his zip lowering had me crying louder, my loud weeping the only sound in the room apart from this bastard's heavy breathing.

He flipped me round so I was facing him, my head shaking at him desperately to stop. He sneered at me. "Ready to be fucked properly? I'll show you how it should be done. Yow owe me this, bitch."

I slapped at him with a hand I'd managed to get free, my other hand dragging over the tiles until a cool bottle touched my fingertips. It was a can of deodorant. I grasped it in my palm, bringing it up and firing across his cheek.

Pain erupted as his knuckles spilt my lip, the blood spraying across his stomach from the force of his hit. My tears stung the wound, the salt biting and stinging.

I was sure I felt my cheekbone fracture when he punched me again, the throb unbelievably hot. My hand fell, the can clanking and rolling out of my reach straight into his.

My back slid across the floor when he thrust the object inside me. I was so dry, the fill of the intrusion ripped me apart, fire igniting and tearing through me. I screamed, causing him to clamp his hand over my mouth, cutting off my nose at the same time. "Like to play with toys, Star? How does that fucking feel?"

Everything became blurry as he suffocated me, his hand pushing harder into my face the more frantic his thrusting became. My hands flapped as I became despondent and weak. I didn't want to die with him violating me. It hurt so much. How cruel must I have been in my past life to deserve this punishment? Vomit curled and I panicked. I would choke to death on my own sick.

Time stilled as everything became surreal. I seemed to float above myself, the world below me, and the air too thin to ground me. My eyes rolled into the back of my head as a smile touched my lips when my life flashed before me in snaps of images so quick I struggled to keep up with them. Momma swung her hand in mine. Daddy taking pictures at my graduation. Jennifer, my best friend, winking as she passed me the bottle of tequila we'd sneaked from her parent's liquor cabinet. A party somewhere unknown, revelers singing Auld Lang Syne. A beach, the sun burning my naked body, someone's lips gently idolizing my bareness. A ring sliding onto my finger via a thread wrapped around my finger and… *HIS.*

I gasped, air filling my lungs too quickly when Theo disappeared from me, the sudden weight loss causing my lungs to inflate rapidly, claiming their fill as swiftly as they could. I rolled over, coughing and spluttering.

"GET OUT OF HERE! HE WILL KILL YOU FOR THIS!" Malik roared.

Nothing felt real. Everything was blurred and dreamlike. I was moving, my body floating through the air. My heart rate had slowed down to a random thump inside my chest as blood roared around my body causing dizziness and light-headedness.

"Ssh," his voice soothed as my sobs wrenched my chest when a current of water covered me. Its torrent slammed against my face, smarting the throb in my cheek and biting the cut to my lip.

I couldn't control the raging weep that tore my chest in two. I couldn't control anything; my breathing, my thoughts, the vomit that surged from me.

"Okay," his soft voice echoed in my head. "I've got you now. I'm so sorry, Star. I just went to the bathroom."

I screamed, punching out at him. "This is your fault! This is all your fault. You did this. You let this happen. You let him do that. No…"

"I'm sorry, Star! Dante will kill him for this."

I continued to abuse him, my fists pounding on his chest, the sopping material of his t-shirt tearing beneath my fingers as I clawed at him. I had finally lost it. Gone mad with it all.

"He's a bastard. You're all fucking evil. Let me go! Please! No more." I scratched at him, my nails digging into his flesh as I tried to tear him to pieces. "I hate you, I hate him. I HATE THIS! SAVE ME PLEASE. SOMEONE SAVE ME!"

Unconsciousness finally won when my mind shut down from the horror of what my life had become.

CHAPTER 14

RAGE

Dante

MY PHONE CONSTANTLY VIBRATING AGAINST my thigh distracted me from the business meeting I was in. These new drug test studies were intriguing a lot of medical boards and all the corrupt players of the black market.

The man sat across from me in his black Armani suit, no tie, slicked back black hair and predatory eyes was just one of the many human traffickers interested in the qualities this new drug possessed. I wasn't in his trade; I made my fortunes the legit way but with fortune, success and science mixed with my own flavor of depravities came the underworld of the black market. Drug trafficking. Human trafficking and all the trash in between. It was inevitable for someone like me to become part of this world and when I did it gave me a power I craved.

The woman he brought with him to the dinner was clearly there to satisfy any desires I may have. A pawn to sweeten the business bond. She was far from my taste. It wasn't the blonde of her hair, I usually favored brunette, it wasn't even the thin frame and ridiculous fake tits cemented to her chest. It was the fact Star had fucked with my hard on; it didn't want to play with any toy but her.

I needed to rectify this. I couldn't have her holding any power over me and I had come too far in this game to break now before the time was right.

"You see, some slaves are easier to break than others." His hand gripped the female's hair and coaxed her to drop beneath the table. "When they start off as trash they welcome a new life, but the expensive top quality pussy tend to be tougher. They like their lives."

His pitch was void in my mind anyway. I had made my deal; it was all set in motion.

Small hands delicately undid my slacks with ease. Her palm reached in to stroke at my flaccid cock. She was working me with experienced hands, trained to only please her Masters. I needed to see Star, watching her locked in her room while someone else got me off would help with the hard on issue.

Slipping my phone free, I typed in the security codes to access the cameras. Her room was empty. It was then I noticed the amount of missed calls and texts.

"Where is she?" My voice bellowed through the corridor to Malik who rushed towards me. "I moved her to your quarters. He messed her up bad. I can't believe I let this happen"

"I'll deal with you later. Where is he?" Not much scared Malik; he was a tank, ex-military. He knew what my wrath was capable of, his wary eyes and posture were one of instinct when sensing a threat much more dangerous.

"He's in his room. Maria is with him." Maria was his woman, only brought in to play a role but she was a parasite; her goal was to be a pillow whisperer to someone like me.

My strides ate up the space to his room. He rose from his sitting position, flanked by Maria. I slipped out my 9mm, swiftly aiming and firing. She dropped like an anchor being dropped in the ocean. Theo's wild eyes scanned my face.

"You had the audacity to touch a woman who belongs to ME!"

He was shaking, the little weasel.

It took me two seconds to locate a can of deodorant. He cried, begging, which I muffled by ramming the entire thing in his mouth, dislocating his jaw with sheer strength as I leaned back and stamped down with my foot, pushing the can down his throat. I watched fear rape him before his lungs failed him - then his heart.

"She is mine!"

"You killed them both." I turned my cold gaze on Malik. "Revenge doesn't like company. Three was a fucking crowd. Let this be a lesson to you."

CHAPTER 15

DIRTY

Star

I WANTED TO SHOWER FROM the inside out. I felt so dirty and broken. My face throbbed in a matching thump to the burning pulse between my thighs. I was completely done, I couldn't take it. I came to the conclusion that although I had proven to adjust to circumstance, cold ruthless violence was not something I could handle.

My internal war still raged with my feelings towards the man I knew as Mr. Troy, who they called Dante. I felt betrayed by him. He let this happen after I willingly gave myself to him. I obeyed his rules and he left me to be violated. God, did he even care? I highly doubted it.

The soft fabric beneath me both soothed and irritated the scratches I knew painted my back. The room was luxury at its finest; silk bedding ornamenting a thick hand-carved four poster solid wood bed. The wood of the furniture, including the floor, was dark in contrast to the white walls and drapes.

A moan escaped me when I tried to sit up, the pressure in my jaw from using the muscles to tilt my head exploded, leaving a wake of pins and needle down the entire side of my face and neck.

"Don't try to move, Belle." His voice was thick and deep, startling me. I hadn't realized he was in the room.

A shadow moved across the room, alerting me to him before his powerful frame filled my sight. He was wearing a white shirt and slacks, a tie undone and hanging in two strips down either side of his chest. I wanted to open my mouth to talk to him but couldn't from the sheer pain.

"You need to not talk or move, Belle. You're extremely bruised and need time to heal. I won't apologize for his actions, those were all his, but I will tell you he paid for them with his life. I don't tolerate disobedience and disrespect from anyone, and you belong to me therefore touching you was directly insulting me."

I wanted to let the bile scorching my throat ignite and decimate me into ash. He didn't give a shit that I was raped with a fucking object or that I couldn't speak through the injuries of callous violence from a man he left me with. I didn't know why I was surprised and hurt by it but I felt it so deeply, the betrayal, and he wouldn't even say he felt bad that it took place.

Closing my eyes, I tried to ward off the coming tears. They were an all too familiar sensation for me, welling and slipping free down my face, collecting in tiny pools at my hair.

I felt his shadow fall over me before his breath warmed my face. My eyes dragged slowly open, his intense features masked by the distortion of my tears. "Everything is not always what it seems, Belle, but you are too weak to learn truths. Sleep now." Pressure pushed down on my lip making me wince, the warm damp swipe of his tongue over the cut soothed the sting.

My eyes pinched closed. I didn't want to feel anyone over me ever again. I would not admit the longing in my chest, though, for him to hold me while I cried a stream of broken tears into him.

I dug my nail into the flesh at the top of my thigh. The sharp sting wasn't as startling anymore. This was the fourteenth indent on my thigh - to count the times the sun had risen while I had been in that room. The outside world was blocked by heavy wooden shutters on the window but the light bled through the cracks just enough to tell me it was day.

My limbs were sore, a weird contradiction to the fact I hadn't used the muscles in them for two weeks. I was on bed rest, a tube inserted to feed me for the first week because my mouth couldn't open; medicine in a drip to make me drowsy and sleep nearly the entire time.

Dante, Mr. Troy, would visit me in my sleepy state, staring at me, clenching his fists. It should have scared me but it didn't, it helped take away the nightmares of that wretched little man touching me. Malik hadn't been permitted to enter the room. I had seen no one and now the walls were closing in on me, cabin fever playing with my mind, my eyesight. I yearned to see and feel the sun. I wanted to feel the warmth cradle me in its embrace.

I turned to the door when I heard footsteps approach. The handle gave way to Dante pushing through the door. He stopped his approach when he saw I was out of bed. He stood there staring at me, making me fidget. I looked down at the gown I was wearing to make sure I wasn't showing any skin to warrant his eyes on me.

"Hey," I awkwardly said, raising a hand before quickly lowering it.

"Do you know who I am?" What kind of question was that? Shit, was this a test, did he know I knew his first name now?

"Mr. Troy," I answered meekly. His eyes flashed with something I couldn't decipher. My stomach began its usual nervous flutter. "Dante," I whispered.

He exhaled and rushed towards me, bundling me up in a bear hug. The restraint from his tight grip made breathing impossible. "You remember. Oh baby, you remember."

Dreaming, I had to be dreaming. Damn these vivid dreams.

His grasp loosened, moving from my back to clasp my face. His lips kissed mine. "You remember." It wasn't a question and the hope in his voice left me completely confused.

My stone posture must have given away the fact I was lost. He stopped his gentle kisses to search my eyes. The door opened again. A female entered. I was hallucinating or dreaming; there wasn't another explanation.

"She still doesn't remember." His words were choked.

"Give her a few more days, Dante."

His posture emanated fury as he turned to her, his body rigid and almost vibrating. "It's been two fucking weeks, Delia!"

What was happening?

"Hello, Star. Can you tell me if you recognize me?"

I looked over the woman. She was attractive, in her thirties if I'd had to guess. She was shorter than me by a couple of inches but her high stilettos gave her extra height. Brown hair was pulled neatly back and placed in low bun. She wore a pencil skirt, and a white doctor's coat open to reveal a satin blouse. She was completely foreign to me with no feeling of familiarity. "No," I uttered.

Her head dropped to a folder in her hands that I hadn't noticed she was holding. "Okay, well my name is Delia; we are actually friends, Star." She smiled like that was all it would take for me to be fine with her statement. "I'm going to have Malik bring you some clothes to pop on and then me and Dante will be back to talk to you."

What the hell?

Moments later I was left on my own again to wonder if that all really took place. Malik entered with a knock to alert me to his presence. Why was everyone acting all civilized all of a sudden? He smiled over at me, placing some jeans and a tee on the bed without a word and then leaving again.

I immediately went to the clothes and ran to the bathroom to put them on. It was such a small thing we all take for granted but to be in normal clothes made me feel human again. The fit was perfect although the items weren't new. It was as if they were bought specifically for my dimensions.

I was wary of the whole change in everything. This beautiful room such a contrast to the cell I'd lived in before the assault. Was it all to lead me into a false sense of security? Before I could let my mind drive me anymore crazy I heard people re-enter the bedroom.

Cautiously I slipped out of the bathroom. The hairs on the back of my neck rose like a wild cat's in the outback, preparing itself, when Dante stood stock still, penetrating me with his eyes, flanked by Delia.

"Star, would you mind coming with us please?" the woman asked.

I flicked my gaze between the two. "Where?" My nerves were going to kill me. I could feel my heart's slow thud echo through my body as if I was hollow, taunting me to the emptiness inside me.

"Just to another room where we can all sit."

Okay, that didn't sound too horrifying unless it was a ruse. Dante turned and exited the room first. Delia gestured for me to following behind him.

We were in a house, the dark wooden theme from the bedroom continuing throughout the entire mass structure. How was it possible that this and my previous prison was the same place? Sensing my thoughts Dante's baritone voice punctured the air. "You were moved when you fell unconscious. This is our house."

Ours? Did he mean his and Delia's? Was he married? Oh God, I felt sicker than ever before.

The hall we were currently passing through opened up into a beautiful living space, a mass of seating choice with a beautiful wooden desk and bookshelves adorning the entire back wall. The neutral colors gave the place an airy feel and for the first time since waking in that cell with no memory, I was looking at a window with rays from the sun dancing through the open blinds. It was like a child first seeing the ocean.

My steps carried me in its direction, summoning me to embrace its touch. It travelled over my feet then up my legs, waist and chest before heating my face. Closing my eyes, I felt the tears prick my lashes. All I was capable of in that moment was inhaling and exhaling, breathing as my body rejoiced in something so simple.

"Star, come and sit, we have a lot to discuss." I swallowed down the sorrow, mourning the light as the shadows dispersed its glow when

I moved into the room to sit at a table with them both. "As I mentioned before my name is Delia, and I consider myself a friend of yours." I didn't speak, just stared straight at her waiting for what more she would tell me. However I wasn't prepared for her next confession. "I work for your fiancé."

Cue the stampede of horses trampling all over my insides. The room dropped out of focus but flooded back in when Dante's hand reached across the table to grasp mine. In slow motion my head turned to him. He was... smiling at me.

"Dante and you asked me to assist you both in a project."

"Fantasy," Dante cut in.

She grinned at him before continuing. "A fantasy, you had, Star."

The buzzing in my ears grew with intensity. She wasn't making sense. Nothing made sense.

"Baby." Flinching from his endearment, I snatched my hand away to cradle it to my chest. My eyes frantically searched them both, begging for them to stop talking in riddles. "The drugs that keep your memory were supposed to wear off but for some reason we're not quite sure of yet, yours hasn't." They drugged me to steal my memories? Was that possible? "My company made a drug to suppress memories. It's used for victims of violent crimes. To help them heal, come to terms slowly with what happened to them. The drug wears off, feeding your memory back little by little."

I couldn't comprehend what I was hearing. They used a drug meant for helping victims of violent crimes, to commit a violent crime. I must have voiced my thoughts because Delia answered me

"Dante is your fiancé, Star. He loves you immensely and finally gave into *your* desires to play out this fantasy."

No, no, no Dante and me? No. No! "You're lying! Who would ever want that? I was kidnapped, humiliated, hit, starved of basic human affection until I craved it. I was RAPED!" The scream tore at the tendons in my throat.

Fury rolled from Dante, physically altering the air around us. "That was never supposed to happen. He was your choice, you trusted him, Star! I knew his woman was interested in me but you trusted that man with everything. I will never forgive myself for such a dramatic lapse in judgment and he paid for it. No one touches what belongs to me and I

know you can't remember this right now but you do be'
I need you back. So look real deep inside that heart of
feel me there. Your body already accepts this otherwi
never given yourself to me."

This was all too surreal. I couldn't stand them looking at m
they were waiting for me to click my fingers and suddenly believe what
they were telling me.

My eyes scanned the room, anything to not look at him waiting
with need for me to tell him … what? I stood with haste, almost knocking my chair over when my eyes came to rest on a huge picture I hadn't
noticed when I first entered the room, too enthralled with the sun. It was
me laying on a beach with…Dante. The smile on my face was natural.
I looked happy, in love.

My legs backed up. It wasn't until a wall met my back and I slowly
slid down until my knees rose to my chest, my arms wrapping around
them, that my mind caught up with my shock. This wasn't true, this
wasn't me. This wasn't real.

CHAPTER 16

SHOCK

Star

A THOUSAND ICE PELLETS HIT me, robbing me of breath and making my skin shrivel in agony. My clothes were instantly drenched and stuck to me like a second skin. My startled scream echoed around the shower cubicle I stood in. The ice pellets turned to warm rain, tapping over my skin. It was then I realized I was actually being held. Strong, arms encompassed my waist and chest, the heat from his body pushed against my back, soothing me.

Breathing in my ear brought me down from the shock I was in. "I'm sorry but you went catatonic, you weren't responding." His arms loosened so I could turn to face him. His expression was full of both pain and anger, his need for me to understand almost suffocating me. "I'm so sorry, baby. I never wanted to go through with this. It was too extreme but it was a fantasy you had and I promised to make every fantasy come true leading up to the biggest one of all. Our wedding."

The water poured down on me, soaking into my skin. I wished with it came my memories, the truth of who I was.

"Why would I want that? To be fucked in front of an audience by someone I don't know?" My tone was accusing and bitter but that was how I felt. No matter what someone tells you is you, to not have any recollection of ever wanting that, it just felt like abuse; physical and now emotional.

"Fuck!" He punched the wall, cracking a few tiles. Blood formed and dripped from abrasions on his knuckles. "I didn't fucking want to do this shit, Star. You did, so I went a little harsher than we discussed but I was pissed at you for wanting that! You belong to me! How could you fantasize about being kidnapped and fucked by the captor?" He was so sincere it was terrifying. "I gave in and gave you what you wanted, and used that little cunt Theo at your request, and he attacked you."

His body slumped back, crashing with the wall and sliding down, his knees coming up to rest his elbows on as he clutched his head in his hands. "After everything, you can't even remember me. I feel like someone ripped my heart out."

I wanted to go to him, crouch down and comfort him but it was all so surreal I couldn't move. I felt cemented to the ground as I watched this dominant man who I thought had bought me and was going to use me as a sex slave break into a shadow of the man I thought him to be. Did he love me? Did I love him?

"I need to dry off." Stupid, irrelevant and random but it was all I could think to say. Dark eyes flashed up to capture mine. He had a way of demanding focus. He was mesmerizing; my urge to go to him when he looked at me was compulsive, engrained into me. My God, there was something about him, always and only him I felt a connection to, my body trying to prompt my mind into remembering.

"The towels are in that cabinet where you keep them. This is your bathroom, Star. You designed it."

My eyes scanned the stone tiles covering every surface. The full mirrors on the back wall overlooked his and hers basins, the mirror had lights around it; it was a feminine bathroom.

"Our room is through the adjoining door. The other space was a spare room I occasionally use." I would question that statement later.

I walked to the cabinet, pulling free a couple of towels, handing one to him before leaving to go into the room he claimed was ours. Floor to ceiling windows made my breath stutter, sheer curtains hung loose, blowing from the gentle breeze seeping through the opening. The natural scent and taste of fresh air is something we all take for granted. Inhaling deep and smiling from the fill of my lungs I sensed him behind me. I slipped the wet clothes from my body so as to not keep dripping on the plush carpet that covered the floor then tucked the towel around me.

White walls and red furnishings colored this room. Rich and warm. There was a dresser littered with perfumes. My feet carried me over to them. Lifting the lid, I smelt each one trying desperately to trigger a memory, a hint of anything about me and my preferences. My fingers brushed over every surface hoping to prompt something but nothing came.

"Your clothes are all in your wardrobe." He pointed to a door. Pushing it open, the heat from his body condensed the air around us. "Here's the switch."

Clothes upon clothes lined the racks; it was bigger than the bathroom. Fancy fabrics, dresses, jackets. "Drawers are where you keep your jeans and tee's," he murmured, gesturing to the drawers built into the bottom of the built in wardrobe.

"Do you mind letting me get dressed?" I meekly asked.

He stared at me, assessing if I was serious then shook his head, lifting his hand in surrender. "Whatever, Star." He pulled the door to, shutting me inside.

I wasn't prepared to feel like the walls were rushing in around me, draining the air from the space. I immediately rushed for the door to open it but it was stiff in my grasp. Panic overcame me, my palm repeatedly crashing down against the wood. "Let me out, let me out. I'm sorry, I'm sorry!"

I staggered forwards when the door gave way.

I landed with a thud into Dante's bare chest. "Ssh, it's okay. I was just letting you change. Ssh." I breathed to the rhythm of his heartbeat, in…out…in…out. I let his calm soak into me. He had tattoos on each arm one reaching over his shoulder. Seeing them was comforting … but why.

"Get changed in here, Star. I'll be in the bathroom, then come down to eat."

I nodded, giving him a hesitant smile. "Thank you."

He shrugged but sighed heavily, his dark eyes catching mine for a moment before he turned and walked away. I watched the way he moved, appreciating the ripple of his back muscles, their bulk showing the sheer strength of him. Frowning to myself, I turned and picked through some clothes, pushing away the ache in my heart.

CHAPTER 17

NORMALCY

Star

I HADN'T GONE DOWN; I stayed in my room. Two weeks I circled the same layout of this room, ignoring his pleas when he brought me food. I couldn't bear it any longer; small images of him kept creeping into my mind like he was summoning me with crumbs of who he was. I missed him and that terrified me.

I could smell pizza when I went in search of him. The aroma became more potent the further into the house I ventured.

He sat at the same table as he had two weeks ago, his hair wet from an impromptu shower I heard him take when I didn't answer his request to come down to eat with him thirty minutes ago. He was dressed casually. I stood out of sight from him but in perfect view to soak him in. In dark loose jeans with a black sweater he still emanated power and dominance; a wolf in sheep's clothing.

I felt it the minute he sensed me there, he had a way of shifting the atmosphere around him. My cheeks heated when he turned in my direction. "Come eat, Belle."

I moved from my not so hidden space, my bare feet tapping over the floor with each step I took. "Why do you call me that?"

He watched me with such intensity, an invisible force wrapped around me like a rope and pulled me closer and closer to him. Standing, cupping my cheek, his minty breath mixed with a hard liquor licked over my skin when he breathed. "Because you have always been the most beautiful woman in a room, the belle of the ball."

Trying not to fidget in his grasp or feel the desire he stoked inside me, I calmly stepped back. His hand dropped with his exhale, and angry eyes pierced me. "You'll have to get used to me touching you, Belle. You are mine, after all. Whether you remember or not that's a fact and something you need to accept!"

I fought back the impending tears. "It's not by choice, not remembering, Dante."

His one stride closed the gap I had put between us. "It was your choice to risk this, Star! Now look what's happened. We're practically strangers who are to be wed in a month." He was grasping my arms in tight fists, making me wince. My stomach chose that moment to grumble, alerting us both to my hunger. I don't know why but I flushed with embarrassment. "I got your favorite."

I looked down at the pizza box. "I don't eat carbs." It slipped through my lips from the woman I was before, shocking us both silent. A glimmer of who I once was came through from nothing. It was small but it was something. His eyes widened, matching my own as my heart sped up. "Oh my God, it just came from nowhere, Dante. But it's true, right?"

A small smile puckered his lips as he nodded. "You have a cheat day once a month and always want pizza; it's your favorite. I took you to Italy so you could have the real thing."

He marched across the room to retrieve a box from the cabinet. He placed it in front of me, removing the lid. Pictures. Lifting the first one I almost dropped it again. There we were together, me smiling up at him as he held the camera out of view, taking the image himself at arm's reach. I looked completely besotted, lovingly gazing up at him. I placed it down on the table and reached for another. I was alone, standing in a field, my hair blowing in the breeze, a smile so bright on my face. I mirrored it, staring down at myself. That was me. Yellow fields spread out behind me like sand in the desert, and perched on a hill, a stunning property overlooked it all. I looked younger though.

"That's our house in the south of France. You were eighteen here." His tone was reminiscent. He took the picture and stroked over the image. "I was so in love with you."

Taking the picture from him, I placed it on the table. "Was?" I held my breath while he intently studied my features before replying.

"She's lost but we will find her again. You're mine Star, you know that. Soon your brain will catch up."

The next picture was of us lying on a sun lounger, him on top of me, nuzzling my neck, my laughter caught perfectly to showcase my happiness. He was so tense beside me. I looked up at him. "This is the holiday when I proposed."

I looked back down at the picture, willing it to tell me our story. I wanted to scream at the girl in there to help me remember, to show me the memories, but nothing came.

Suddenly he grabbed me and smothered my mouth with his. I let him, losing myself to his carnal need. His tongue angrily swiped at mine, his teeth nipping at my lips. His hand dropped down to grasp my ass cheeks, lifting me up against his body. Mine worked without command, everything fluid like muscle memory. My body remembered him, wanted him, craved him and it was the only thing that actually felt real in my life. I needed the anchor he was offering.

He placed me on the table, forcing his way between my parted thighs, the bulge in his jeans rubbing against me to elicit friction hard enough to encourage the arousal to spark. He was all over me, his hands groping my breasts, his cock rubbing against me, his mouth devouring my lips, cheeks, neck. He was animalistic and brutal in his claiming and that was what this was - a hunter claiming his prey.

He lifted my tee from my body, exposing more skin for him to kiss, lick, bite and mark. When his hot mouth closed over my lace covered nipple a flash conjured an image in my head of us making love, slow and intimate, white sheets beneath us, skin to skin, every part of us touching, connecting as if we were one being. I gasped when it faded and reality rushed in. The gentle love making was replaced with the same man pushing me to my back, tearing my jeans down my legs without removing my panties. He pulled them to the side and thrust fully inside me. I hadn't even seen him release his cock from the confines of his jeans.

The rude entry sting eased into wet strokes of pure pleasure. He fit me like a glove, as if I was made to his perfect measurements. There was no doubt in my mind I belonged to him, even without the picture evidence and memory flash of us. My body ignited for him, moved in sync with his, my body remembered that his owned it.

With every rushed thrust my back scraped against the wood beneath me, moving me away only for his hold on my hips to pull me back onto him. The burn in my core exploded, tightening me around him and milking his cock. He roared into the room like the beast he was, pulling from me, hot ribbons of cum squirting from him to soak my stomach and breasts.

Our mixed pants filled the void of silence in the room. "Fuck I love how you feel on my cock. You're such a tight little slut." His words shocked me, even though he had spoken in such a way before, when I believed I was a captive.

He lifted each ankle, placing them on the table so he had a perfect view between my thighs. Ripping the lace away, the cool air licked over the wet juices there. "Your cunt is seeping for me, hungry for more. Look at it pulsing. Swollen pink perfection."

I suddenly felt exposed and vulnerable at his observation of the after effects of my climax. Sickness clawed its way up the back of my throat. It had only been weeks since I was attacked and yet thoughts of that violation didn't filter in when he was touched me, fucked me. That should have been a good thing but mixed with his words, I felt disgusting. But Dante was an artist and his craft... me. I held no restraint or power when it came to him.

"Don't let the bad memories rule you, Star. Let's make new ones." He knew what I was thinking about. His lips came down to suck at my exposed clit. My head dropped back, clashing with the hard planes of the table but the moan was only for the build he grew within me. Fingers plunged into the hot depths of my core as his tongue lapped up every hint of my release. He flicked his tongue over my pink folds using his thumb to circle the hood of my clit. The pressure grew, the firmness pushing down. I was going to explode. His thumb left me so he could slap at my clit. I wanted to tell him no, it was humiliating but the blood rushing to that area, the contrast between his soft wet tongue licking me and his thumb working me too, then the quick, sharp smack had my body in a battle of serene pleasure and pain. The ripples of my orgasm were so intense I screamed as my body convulsed. "Dante! Oh God, yes! Oh God." My nails scraped at the table.

"That's it, Star, fucking cum. Squirt all over me you horny fucking bitch, your pussy loves to be owned. CUM!" The pressure exploded, coating his fingers and mouth in wave after wave of my release. I felt the wetness running down and pooling at my butt cheeks. If I wasn't completely limp in a state of euphoria I would have been embarrassed. "My cock wants to swim in you, Star. You cum like a porn star."

He flipped me onto my front. Raising my ass in the air, he swiped his tongue from the front of my slit and over my throbbing clit, dipping into my core before travelling up the seam of my ass. I wriggled, trying to pull forward but his grip was too strong. His tongue circled the forbidden hole there. His palm came down hard on my ass cheek, making me squeak. "Bring your feet down, Star, so you're bent over the table." I did as he commanded, having to reach up on my tip toes to keep my ass in line with his hips. My breasts squished against the cool wood, giving my sensitive nipples some relief from the ache of needing simulation.

Kicking my ankles to part them, my legs spread wide to give him the access he demanded. Grabbing two handfuls of my ass cheeks, he parted them. The head of his cock leaked pre-cum, making my pussy hungrier for him, the waves of fluttering need begging to be sated.

"Your pussy is a greedy little thing; it needs to learn to share." With that he pushed his way through the ring of muscle, straight inside my ass, making me screech. The pressure was different and although it stung and I wanted to push out the feel of him, there was pleasure.

"You need to warn people, Dante!" I chastised, to only gain a mocking chuckle.

"Belle, your ass loves strangling my cock. Your body remembers me, just let it lead you."

As insane as that was, I did. I let my body remind me of Dante because he was the only grasp on life I had. It was so scary, an abyss inside myself. I needed the comfort of him owning me and he did, the pizza forgotten, the pictures splayed out around us while he gave me new memories. They were brutal but I could touch them.

CHAPTER 18

INFORMATION

Star

"I CAN JUST ORDER A fresh one."

Smiling, I shook my head. "It's fine reheated." I would have eaten the pizza cold at that point. My stomach was going to eat itself soon, I was that hungry. I felt a little awkward, like I had given up sex on a first date, kind of slutty.

He struggled to turn on the oven. There were a million different knobs and it took up nearly half the back wall with numerous burners; it was impressive. "I take it I do the cooking?" I joked, going over to help him.

He stared at me. He did that a lot which made me uneasy. It was like I was the stranger to him not the other way around. "We have a cook but I gave her some time off due to your memory loss." Throwing the box down he stormed past me, making me flinch from the hostility of his demeanor.

Guilt swarmed me; it was my fault this was happening. If I hadn't been so selfish with my own desires and needs, he wouldn't be living with a stranger. Thoughts of everything that had happened raced through my mind. Why, if we were in love enough to get married, would I have been so indulgent to my own needs, enough that I would make him play along and make it happen? What a selfish, horrible person I must have been to force him into that. How could I have ever wanted that? I didn't remember the person I was but surely I would have the same urges as her, and the thought of being held captive and degraded would forever be my worst fear. There was nothing sexually desirable about what I lived through in those last few weeks.

My breath hitched when I thought of Maria. Who was she? And as a fiancé madly in love, how would I ever be okay with my fiancé shoving his dick down her throat?

Opening the box of pizza and grabbing a slice, I followed him, finding him in an office with his head in his hands. I gingerly approached him, nervous of his mood. "I'm sorry." I didn't know what else to say. I hated that I was doing this to him.

His head lifted, his arms reaching out. My body felt the invisible tug. Going to him, I crawled into his lap, curling my legs up and into myself. "I'm sorry."

"It's okay, it will come." I breathed in the whiskey from his breath as he spoke.

"Tell me about everything, Dante. Where was that place you held me?"

Waiting a few silent beats, he paused before he answered. "I have a lab and an office built on some of the property. I'm not one for sharing a work space. I made some remodels to accomplish what you had in mind."

My stomach alerted me to the fact the cold slice of pizza was still in my hand and not my empty stomach. I flushed, a little embarrassed that he heard.

"Let me order fresh. I have someone who brings me what I need."

What did he mean by that? Didn't he just call a pizza house like everyone else? I shook my head and nibbled on the cheese around the crust. "Why did you let Maria… su…do what she did?" I tried to keep the jealously from my tone but I failed, making me wince faintly at my questioning.

He shifted me so my eyes met his. "She was your idea, Star. You said it would make things more believable." I didn't feel like he was talking about me. I hated that he let her do that now I know who he was and what we were.

"Did you do anything else with her?"

His deep laugh rocked my body with his. "You're jealous? She was nothing, Star. I was thinking about you the whole time I was down her throat! And oral was all you would allow. You don't like to share." Now that sounded more like the person I was discovering I was.

"What about the others?"

His postures stiffened. "Malik works for me. I've known him for a very long time and we both trust him impeccably. The other one worked for you and is gone now." A chill raced through me with the sickening feeling that accompanied any thoughts of Theo.

"What do you mean gone?" I had a foggy memory of him telling me Theo had paid with his life but he didn't mean…did he?

His fingers pinched into the flesh of my thigh. "Gone. Don't ask about him again." I heeded his warning; his tone was deadly leaving a shiver to rattle through me.

Rubbing my hand over his to try to loosen his grip, I continued. "What do I do, work wise?"

Cupping my face in his palm, his lips stroked over mine. "You're an artist. It was always your dream. I have some of your work over there."

An artist? Wow! My eyes roamed the walls and stopped on a painting. It was of the house, the one in the south of France, only it was Dante instead of me in the image. It was so lifelike. "What about my family?"

He maneuvered me from his lap briskly, causing me to blink at him in surprise. "You're asking a lot of questions." Fidgeting from foot to foot now he'd removed me from his lap, I felt dejected and nervous. I hated not knowing his limits; hated not knowing the dynamics of us.

"I need answers because everything was erased. I just wondered if I had family," I replied sharply, standing up.

His hands grasped the back of my neck, tilting my face up to his. "I'm your family! That's all you need to know. Now it's been a long day, you need to go rest." He dropped his hold and pointed to the door. Embarrassment colored my cheeks. He was dismissing me like a child, sending me to bed.

I lay awake that night, until my body gave out. But I knew he never came in the room. Nor did he sleep in our bed.

CHAPTER 19

ADAPT

Star

THE HOUSE WAS HUGE, THE many walls, though countless and far apart, still felt claustrophobic in their need to contain me inside something I was unfamiliar with. I needed to get out, find open space, somewhere that would allow me room to breathe and feel free.

Dante had informed me a few hours ago that he would be in his office and I was to reacquaint myself with the house, to explore at my leisure. He laughed, saying I wasn't a prisoner but his humor was lost on me; it was too soon for me to make jokes about everything that had come to pass. I thought walking around the house would help but it was as lonely as it was large. Nothing felt like mine, although my *fiancé* had been insistent that it was. The many pictures of the two of us adorning the walls soothed me in one respect, but they also taunted me, laughing at my inability to remember them.

Sighing, I climbed the wide staircase to the upper floor. Malik walked towards me with a warm smile on his face. His height would have given him an almost gangly appearance if it wasn't for his width.

"Hey. How are you?" His gentle eyes brought a soft sense of comfort.

I shrugged. "I…"

He reached towards me and placed his hand on the top of my arm, rubbing up and down in an effort to quell my unease. "It'll come, Star. Just give it time." Something flashed across his eyes, I couldn't ascertain what it was but I smiled back.

"I know. It's just… hard. I…" Tears filled my eyes and I blinked them back, pushing away the feeling of loneliness.

"Hey." His arms wrapped around me, his warm body giving me reassurance as his chin rested on the top of my head. It felt strange having him be so familiar with me despite the fact he had seen me naked and played a big role in my fake kidnapping. I understood from what Dante had told me that I knew Malik and with only having memories of the few people around me from the past weeks, I felt connected to him and in a weird way. "I can't begin to imagine what you're going through but I know everything will work out."

I nodded, though my words contradicted my optimism. "Will it?"

He sighed then reared back, his eyes flicking up to the camera sat in the corner of the ceiling. "I promise." It was said in a whisper but his eyes held mine for a moment too long. "Dante is demanding more tests to be carried out on the drug they gave you. And I know Dante better than anyone. He'll make sure it's sorted soon."

I narrowed my eyes and tipped my head. "You know him better than I'm supposed to? I thought we were childhood sweethearts."

He chuckled. "You are, Star, but I've been his friend and have worked for him a long time. I know what time he wakes, what he likes for breakfast. Hell, I even know the length of his dick." My eyes widened but he laughed and winked at me. "I have to go, the Master calls."

A shiver racked through my body with his words, and although they were meant in jest, the way he called Dante *Master* prickled something inside me, memories of the last few weeks haunting me. He clicked his tongue and stroked my arm again before disappearing down the stairs. I watched him vanish then turned back and walked towards *our* bedroom.

Even though I'd only taken one step into the room, I hated how foreign it felt. A bedroom was a place of private time, somewhere that should hold many memories but for me it was an unfamiliar square space filled with strange objects. My eyes wandered over the room, trying to get a grasp on something, anything that felt recognizable.

Walking over to the dressing table, I lifted the lid on a small jewelry box. Many sparkling pieces blinked at me when the light hit them. A ring seized my attention and I slid my little finger into it and lifted it closer. It was a stunning piece, a platinum band holding a large chunk of diamond. My eyes widened and a shiver raced over me.

His hand looped a thread around my ring finger. The tears spilled free when I noticed the other end was looped around his own finger, a platinum band with a huge diamond sat on the end of his. He tilted his hand, making the ring flow free down the thread until it looped onto mine. I choked on a happy sob. "Promise never to leave me, to never love another man. Promise to be my wife, promise to complete us?"

A tear slid free and I lowered myself onto the stool. My reflection looked back at me from the mirror fixed to the table, a masked replica, an unknown image of a woman whose life meant nothing to me.

"Who am I?"

Sliding the ring onto my ring finger, I watched it take a repeat journey of what it had done many months ago, begging for the action to bring on further flashbacks but nothing else came, only a deep-seated need for knowledge. My eyes blinked back at me, my tanned skin and flushed cheeks glowed, my soft pink lips parted allowing life to stream in and out of me but I didn't feel alive, I felt dead on the inside. My heart ached as my hollow soul begged for warmth and connection. One thing was for certain though, my spirit was still alive, it's need for me to battle through allowing me to take each step of this new life and keep going. I had no other choice. I didn't have anything to fall back on; or rather I didn't know of anything I had to fall back on. Dante was the only thing that linked me to this world. The photographs and his knowledge about me were the only things that could grant me a vision into my past life.

I blew out a determined breath and gave myself a stern nod. "You have no choice, Star. You have to deal with this. Like Malik said, it'll come, you just have to lean on Dante until it does." I smiled at the echo of myself looking back at me. "He obviously loves you. He gave you a fantasy he didn't want to participate in, he put your needs before his own and if that isn't a sign of love then I don't know what is."

My pep talk gave me the courage to stand and scramble through the huge clothes closet until I found some pumps and slid them on. Air would do me the world of good, maybe a walk through the gardens. I wouldn't trust myself to venture further afield; I couldn't remember my damn name never mind the layout of the estate where we lived.

I secretly hope I had been a keen gardener. I craved to see flowers and greenery. I wasn't sure why I needed to see nature but I did so I shrugged and went with it, smiling faintly at something else I had discovered about myself.

I couldn't move, not that moving would make any difference. My eyes scanned the miles of ocean before me, my heart galloping with the realization that I was completely surrounded by open water. I had walked the entire perimeter around the house to be only greeted with shoreline. How the hell did one get off the island?

Although the crashing waves called to soothe me, they did the exact opposite, bringing terror with each white foamy surge of pure blue water. The vastness of nothing but sea gave me another feeling of confinement, its strangling hold squeezing my insides when I acknowledged the fact that I wasn't going anywhere.

I knew deep inside that Dante loved me, he was my fiancé for Christ's sake, but the feeling that I couldn't have my own space was crippling. I needed time to think, think about what I wanted. But it was as though everything had been decided for me, leaving me no choice but to spend my time with a man I hardly knew. He said I wasn't a prisoner but I was secluded with no escape. To me, that made me a prisoner. My brain was being rational; I wasn't giving him the benefit of the doubt or considering that the old me maybe loved it here, but now it was all building inside me, making me panic.

A large black cloud rolled over my head, forecasting an approaching storm. It matched my mood, the thunder inside my head loud and angry, the roll of electricity surging through my veins and constricting the oxygen racing into my organs. How dare he trap me like this? How dare he be the one to choose where I went?

I spun round. Dante watched me from the base of the crooked stone steps that had brought me to the beach. His eyes were narrow but the slight incline to his head alerted me to the fact that he was also furious. Why, I had no idea.

Storming up the sand, my feet slid into the shingle as my angry steps powered me forward; Dante remained still but intrigued when he sensed my temper.

"Where are we?" I demanded, my tone hot and vile. His brow lifted but he just stared at me. "Tell me, Dante. Where the hell are we? And how do I get off this… this mass of nothing?"

His teeth clenched, his jaw hardening but I observed him trying to control his own anger. "You are home."

"Home? Home? Then why doesn't it feel like home? Why does it feel like a prison?" I struggled to keep the tears at bay, battling with myself not to show any weakness in front of such a controlling, dominant man. "I don't want to be here. Please take me onto land. I'll find a hotel there."

The corner of his lips twitched, amusement now overtaking his rage. "A hotel?" He crossed his arms over his chest and leaned back, resting against a stone wall.

"Yes!" I glared at him. "What the hell is your problem?"

I saw the red mist slithering across his face but I didn't care. I needed some space, time to figure out who I was before I could characterize our relationship.

"My problem," he sighed as he pushed off the wall and took a step towards me. "Is that you are punishing me for giving you everything you ever wanted." I blinked at him as hurt and fury ruled him. "What do you want from me, Star? You begged me, pleaded with me to give in to your fantasy, your sordid side. You threatened to leave me, damn it!"

My eyes widened and my mouth fell open, shock rendering me speechless as I watched him finally let free his anger with me. "I…"

"You?" he barked as he stepped into me. "You! It's always fucking you isn't it, Star? You're so selfish. Fuck! I gave up everything for you, even my damn dignity. You forced me to degrade you in front of others. Have you any idea how that made me feel?"

I shook my head, my neck bent backwards as I looked up at him. "I'm… I'm sorry. I didn't realize."

He screwed up his face, running his fingers through his hair in agitation. "Christ, Star. I don't know what to do to help you, to help us anymore. I feel like I've lost you. You aren't mine anymore, you're… you're this empty shell, this beautiful fucking woman who has slipped into the sea and drowned, leaving behind an echo of what she was."

My heart beat frantically. I had no idea he felt that way. I had put my own selfish feelings first, disregarding how he would feel about all this. And if it had really been me that had asked for this… fantasy, then there was no one to blame but myself.

Reaching out with my hand, I slid my fingers through his, linking our palms together. "I'm sorry, Dante. I… I'm being selfish. I have no idea how I'm supposed to feel. I don't even remember my emotions. It's so hard and… and I need you to help me through this."

I did need him because he was all I had. He was the only memory that had been granted to me, albeit a small flash of memory but it was definitely him, the only thing locking me to myself.

He closed his eyes and exhaled deeply, worry tightening his face. "I know, Star." He leaned down, resting his forehead against mine. "I know you remember nothing about yourself. But believe me, I'm your past." His soft lips ventured down the bridge of my nose, his warm breath seeping into my skin and warming me inside. "Let me be your future."

I released my hands from his and brought them to cup his face. "Show me. Make me feel you again."

He moaned, a choked sound rippling from his chest before he gently pressed his lips to mine. His tender kiss was full of emotion, almost suffocating me as he controlled me and begged me with connection to let him in. Sliding my hands into his thick hair, I grasped at him, pulling him hard against me. My body ignited, roared for him. The heat he fired in me was always unbearable, difficult to breathe through. His strong arms wrapped me up, drawing me closer to him.

"Star," he breathed as his lips dampened a trail down the edge of my neck, his tongue tasting me as his parted lips led the way. "You've always been mine, baby. Always. I'll never set you free."

I frowned at his need but forced his face back up so I could kiss him again. My back pressed against the wall when he turned us. He palmed my backside, lifting me until I clamped my legs around his waist and used him for support when my body liquefied in his passion. Taking my hands in one of his, he sandwiched them between our chests. His tongue twisted around mine as desire curled around us. His breaths into my mouth were heavy and heated, matching my own as want took control.

Dante suddenly gasped and pulled away then looked down at our hands. His eyes locked onto the ring adorning my finger. He brushed the tip of his finger over it, his face darkening but his eyes moistening.

"Hey." He blinked at me, pain enveloping him. "What's wrong? I thought wearing it would please you."

He gulped and nodded stiffly. "Yeah it does It... It just shocked me to see you wearing it. You didn't waste any time, did you?"

I frowned at his sudden anger. "I'm sorry." I snatched my hand back and yanked at the band, pulling it from my finger. "I'm sorry." He stared at me as I flung it at him. "I can't figure you out."

What the hell had I done wrong now? Everything was so confusing. Trying to please him always had the opposite effect and I was tired of trying.

I ran up the steps towards the house, refusing to look back to see if he was following. Fuck him and his crazy moods.

I squealed when I was suddenly lifted high, my body jolting when I was slung over Dante's shoulder. "Calm your shit, Belle. You need to learn to control that damn temper of yours. You've been too spoilt."

"What?" I scoffed as I pushed against his back, trying to force myself free from him.

"Don't fight with me, Star. You won't like who wins the battle."

Amazement rendered me frozen. What the hell? I couldn't keep up with him. "Let me go, Dante!"

"Not until you learn a lesson from your behavior."

"What?" I sounded like a stuck record, repeating the same word over and over but my shocked brain couldn't figure out what else it wanted to say.

"It's time to find out who rules this relationship, *Belle*. I don't put up with hissy fits from you!" His tone was derisive and mocking, making my stomach churn.

"What do you mean?" I struggled in his hold, striving to escape but it was impossible, he was too powerful.

He stormed through the house, his fury at me eating up the atmosphere around us. I couldn't understand what I had done wrong, apart from wearing our engagement ring, then slinging it back at him when he took offence to me wearing it.

"Dante, please. You're scaring me."

He chuckled. "Good, maybe the old you is in there after all."

What the hell did that mean? Why would the old me have been scared of him?

A chill slithered over me at the tone in his voice. He'd morphed into someone else on our journey through the house. He was relentless in his pursuit to get to where he wanted, his steps never slowing or faltering.

We marched through new corridors I hadn't seen before, slipping through numerous doors, descending several steps and floors until we came out into a long hallway, stone brickwork the only décor on the walls. A coolness seeped into us, heightening my fear and amplifying Dante's rage.

"Dante. I'm scared." He ignored me. Tears burned the back of my eyes as I struggled harder in his grasp. "Let me go, Dante!"

He kicked out at a heavy wooden door; however, it didn't move but when he stabbed at a keypad beside the door, I realized he had kicked it in temper, not to open it. He stalked forward through the now open doorway, his actions furious and controlled, terrifying and disturbing.

He pulled me away from his body, placing my feet on the floor before spinning me round so I could view the room we had ended our journey in.

My knees buckled. My breath left my body in a single forceful rush. My skin prickled, each tiny hair rising in horror as my heart threatened to hammer out of my chest.

Hell greeted me. Emptiness apart from what looked like a table against the back wall, stone walls and nothing in between. A cell. Oh God, another cell. He was going to lock me up!

I raced for the door but he grabbed my arm, stopping my departure. "Calm down."

I was shaking all over. "Please don't leave me in here."

Amusement colored his features. "Oh I'm not leaving you, quite the opposite. Take your clothes off, Belle. You need to know who you belong to, who owns every part of you and that you never want to leave."

My pulse quickened with his words. There was no doubt who owned my body, it awakened and succumbed to his voice, presence, commands. The scared feeling vanished and left pure anticipation.

He moved us further into the room, it was then I noticed the huge stone fireplace with a beautiful gold framed mirror above it. My feet carried me towards it, stopping when I stubbed my toes. "Ouch!" I squeaked, looking down at what I kicked. Iron restraints were bolted to the floor. My eyes grew wide, my head spinning to lock on to Dante. His sinister smirk made my stomach drop.

"Clothes, Belle. Fucking lose them."

Swallowing, I began to strip away the layers, the cold air nipping across my flesh and pebbling my nipples. I startled from the loud hiss and crackle of the fire Dante had switched on. The flames cast shadows over the walls, cloaking over his form and making him look even more devastatingly beautiful and dangerous.

I slipped my panties down my legs to join the pile at my feet. He kicked them aside, dropping down in front of me, guiding my foot into the iron cuff and locking it around my ankle before repeating with the other foot. I attempted to shift my feet that were now restrained with only a small gap between them but there was no give. I was bound to the spot.

My breath became heavy, my chest lifting and falling to the rhythm of my thundering heartbeat. Licking the pads of two fingers, Dante traced them up my inner thigh, the heat from the fire making his path tickle and excite. In almost a whisper of a touch, he stroked them up my slit then blew against my pussy, its delicate but precise wisp making my insides ignite. His palms splayed on my navel, skimming over my skin and up to my heavy breasts. Cupping them, he lifted slowly, his mouth opened, inhaling my scent, the bristles from his growth of stubble pricked at my sensitive flesh.

My hands reached into his thick hair, tugging to lift him to my needy nipples. I needed to feel his mouth there. He allowed me to guide him, his lips closing over one puckered bud. His urgent strokes from his tongue and sharp suck nearly made my legs give out. His teeth bit down, the harsh sting, then the smooth laps contradicting each other.

My moans echoed around us, hitting the empty air and rebounding from the walls to make a chorus of pleasure cries. His mouth sucked my nipple harder before abandoning me with a loud pop. I mourned the loss of his warm, strong body and teasing lips. A palm coming down hard on my ass made me whimper. His chuckle followed him around the room as he stalked over to the table. Lifting it effortlessly, he brought it over to me, placing it in front of me a few feet from my body.

My brow lifted with curiosity when he gestured to the table. "Lean forward, Belle. Place your hands on the table."

Biting my lip to try and instill some calm into my raging body, I did as he asked, leaving my ass prone, the cooler air gaining access to my now exposed pussy lips. Once my hands were placed firmly on the cool surface, he began to pull the table further away, forcing my body to bend further forward with every inch he moved it. My arms outstretched fully, so much so that I would have struggled to right myself. He grinned when he saw that conclusion flitter across my face.

Walking away from me, I heard a chain rattle behind me. I tilted my head to try and steal a glimpse of what he is doing. Two huge ringed iron hoops hung from the ceiling about six feet apart with a length of dark red material looped through one, dipping in the empty space between before looping through the other. How had I not noticed them before? The chain noise was him pulling a chain attached to another ring on the wall. With each pull the material lowered.

"You need to learn that your body, your soul, your life is all mine for taking if I so wish it. But you also need to learn to trust me." My neck hurt from craning to look at him, his hand reaching for the gaping fabric. He began walking back towards me. "You gave me your soul a long time ago, Star. You'll learn who you belong to again. You'll learn that this isn't a prison, it's your freedom. You give yourself to me completely and trust me when I say I take it!" With that he lifted the red silk over my head, resting it against my throat, the cool smooth feel caressed my skin.

He moved away again, the sound of the chain clanking once more filling the quietness. The silk lost its slackness with every toll of the chain, pulling tight against my throat, forcing me to hold my head looking straight ahead. There was a small amount of give but not much. If I was to step forward I would choke and stepping anywhere was impossible anyway. I was completely at the mercy of the table holding my weight and the silk wrap encasing my throat, my life.

My eyes found my own reflection in the mirror. I could see Dante standing behind me. I should have remembered the mirror was there but my brain was a mass of mush. I couldn't think straight, endorphins flooding my system.

His clothes joined mine on the floor and I took a few moments to soak in the glorious body he boasted. His impressive chest was strong and wide, defined abs rippled down to the indentations of his V, like an arrow pointing me to the hard smooth velvet of his cock. I could feel my excitement dampen my pussy lips. The heat from the fire licked over my face and chest.

His hands came down on my ass, slightly spreading the cheeks, the wet head of his cock nudging at my entry before plunging straight into my core. The silk gripped me in its hold as my body jolted forwards, my eyes watering from the restriction, my breathing labored.

His firm grip on my ass pulled me down onto him with his every thrust forward, hitting the sweet bundle of nerves deep inside and pushing me to the brink of strangulation. "Feel how close to the edge of life and death you are, Belle. Your lungs beg for air yet your pussy screams for my cock. You're where you're supposed to be, with me inside you."

His hips powered forwards, the heat inside me clawing from the pit of my stomach and expanding throughout my entire being. I felt his hand slip between my legs to pinch and slap at my clit. I exploded in a torrent of pleasure ripples, gasping to fill my body with the air it desperately sought. The lack of oxygen left me lightheaded and in a state of semi-consciousness. I felt like I was floating, flying.

"Dante!" I choked out as my pussy closed in around his hard cock, soaking him in my climax. His arm wrapped around my waist to assist my weak legs, holding my body from falling.

"Feel me, baby. Feel how I own you in every sense of the word."

CHAPTER 20

SEX

Dante

SHE WAS STUNNING IN HER euphoria. She had always been driven by her sexual cravings, her body ruling her mind throughout her life. It was why we worked, because she fed my needs and I hers.

I missed her but it was like learning about the girl I fell in love with all those years ago all over again. There was a time when I'm inside her, buried in all the flawlessness, that I wish I could erase my memories and let us both start from scratch, fall in love again but I would never allow that.

After bringing her down from her high, releasing her from the confines, she passed out in my arms, sexually sated and weak.

Making my way to my office, my steps faltered when I saw Malik in there. His eyes were transfixed on the monitor to which the silk room was displayed through the camera hidden in the mirror.

"Malik!" I barked, making him jump.

"Shit, you scared me."

Clearly, the prick!

"What the fuck are you doing in here, watching that room?"

He shifted, stalling to answer. I beat down the impending urge to choke him until he answered. "It's my job to monitor the house cameras." He shrugged.

I pinned him with a deadly glare before stalking towards him. Leaning over the desk, I inhaled deeply. "She's mine and your interest isn't going unnoticed. I warn you now. Lose it!"

His eyes widened. Standing, he held his hand up. "Lose what?" he fumbled to say.

I prodded my finger in his chest. "Any temptation to watch us, to butt your nose in to business not concerning you. I won't warn you again. You forget your place. Now get the fuck out my office."

Dropping his eyes to the floor, he dragged himself from my office. The cunt needed to find a woman to get off on. I snatched up my cell and dialed Hunter's number. He could come to dinner, bring a few dinner guests, one to milk Malik's cock for him. It would be good for Star to see that my friends knew where she belonged and that she should accept her place with me instead of acting like a brat.

CHAPTER 21

ACQUAINTANCES

Star

HIS EYES SIMMERED AS THEY roamed over me. I gulped at the intense lust he radiated. Looking down on myself, trying to see me as he saw me, I smiled and ran my palms over the deep red silk. It occurred to me when I had seen the dress laid out on the bed for me to wear that it matched the red silk in the basement he had taken me in earlier. To say that my body had not only succumbed to him but had come to life under him was an understatement.

My memories wouldn't allow me to compare him to past lovers but I knew the connection we had sexually was powerful, both of us feeding each other as we consumed what the other gave.

He stalked across the room towards me, making me bring my gaze back to him. His expression was stern and it made me shiver. His finger gently tipped my chin back so my eyes were secured under his own stare. "Red suits you. However, it makes me want to spoil your perfection. Incites in me the need to break you."

My eyes widened. "Do you want me to change?"

He smirked at me, his hand now sliding down the front of me, his finger dipping into the cleavage my underwear produced. "I want to tear you out of it and fuck you until you drown in your own climax."

I nodded slowly, my heart galloping as my womb squealed in delight, demanding that he perform his declaration. I swallowed the lump that had formed in my throat and licked at my dry lips. "Perhaps I should keep it on then."

His own eyes widened at my bold tease. "Patience heightens the pleasure, Belle. I promise to make the wait worthwhile." I had no doubt he would keep his promise.

He took a step back and held out his hand. Slipping my fingers through his, he curled his own around mine and led me from the room.

"I'm quite nervous," I said.

He glanced at me but kept moving, my feet scurrying alongside him to keep up with his wide strides. "Of?"

"Well, your friends. Meeting them."

He sighed and pursed his lips as if angry with my admission. "*Our friends*. This will be around the hundredth time you have *met* them, Star. For fuck's sake, they were at our freaking engagement party. We holidayed in Vegas with Hunter and his then girlfriend. We spent last Christmas with Garth."

"I'm sorry," I said with a small nod.

He sighed heavily and pulled to a stop. "No, I'm sorry, baby. I should learn some of that patience I was talking about."

I smiled softly at his remorse. "We both need to consider one another's difficulty in this."

Kissing me gently on the forehead he pulled me the remaining distance to the room our guests were situated in.

I followed him into the space, my eyes widening on what welcomed me. Three men chatted between themselves, but it wasn't them who had grabbed my attention, it was the women accompanying them. Each was model worthy, their figures and looks simply striking. However, it wasn't their looks that made me stare, it was the way they stood, each by the side of their men, each face lowered to the floor, each as submissive as the next. Although I often considered myself naive, I recognized 'toys' when I saw them.

All heads turned in our direction, every single eye in the room coming to rest on me. I twitched nervously beside Dante, my fingers tightening my hold on him. His clutch gently increased, supporting me when it was obvious to him my nerves were getting the better of me.

One of the men grinned widely and instantly strolled over to us. He stood before me, his grin turning to a soft smile. "Star."

I glanced up at Dante in confusion. "Hunter," he revealed.

"Oh." I smiled up at the tall man, his thick mane of dirty blonde hair a contrast to the dark stubble on his chin. "We shared vacations."

He smiled widely and nodded. "Vegas. Such fun." I frowned at the twinkle in his eye, a hint of mischief evident. "You gave us quite a scare, sweetheart."

Dante stiffened beside me with Hunter's endearment but Hunter rolled his eyes. "Oh relax, Troy."

I felt eyes burning through me, and turning towards the stare my body tensed at one particular girl; she couldn't have been any older than eighteen. Her eyes were pinched, her stare on me intense and if I read her correctly, shock widened her pupils.

I dropped my eyes to my body, checking for rips in the fabric or splashes of perfume that had left stains but I couldn't see anything. The hairs on the back of my neck were alert and frigid with the potency of her gawp. I shivered causing Dante to look at what held my attention. His own eyes narrowed as she continued to stare at me. I was growing uncomfortable, sure there was something wrong with me, something warranting her rudeness.

"What's with your date?" Dante asked.

Hunter turned to see what Dante was referring to. He frowned then ventured over to her, grabbing her arm and pulling her to one side.

"She gives me the jitters."

Dante chuckled and pulled me close to his side. "Don't worry, my princess. Your knight will save you from the dragon's evil intentions."

I giggled. Dante's face lit up and he gazed at me with a soft smile. "Now that's something I have missed."

"Dante!" Malik shouted from across the room. I hadn't realized he had joined us until he stepped out from behind a curvy girl. He smiled at me, his eyes lighting up when he looked over my dress. I noticed Dante's footing stutter when he caught Malik's perusal.

"Star?" I smiled and nodded at the man who had appeared on my right. He snatched my hand and lifted it to his mouth, kissing my knuckles softly. "Garth. You probably don't remember me. It was quite some time ago."

I squinted at him.

The ball sailed through the air, gaining velocity the closer it got to me. I scuttled backwards, the back of my leg slamming into the bleachers as I attempted to shift myself from its destination. The hum of noise it produced with the speed it came made me squeal before it actually reached me.

Laughter erupted when it whizzed past my ear, marginally missing me but whipping my hair up and gluing to my face with the heat from the summer sun.

Dante jogged over to me, his teenage face bright and red with laughter. "Baby." He laughed. "Are you okay?"

A few other friends ran over to us. "Shit. I'm so sorry." Garth stared at me with a guilty grimace. I reached over and slapped at him.

"Do I look like a goal post?"

Everyone started with the hysterics again as Dante pulled me into his firm body. "I can guarantee you are nothing like a pole."

My jaw dropped as the boys hissed and whistled. "Are you calling me fat?"

"What?" He shook his head quickly. "No. No!"

I winked at him then reached up to kiss him on the cheek. "Although, I must say, I'm rather partial to your long pole."

I thought I'd managed to say it quietly but from the whistles and prods in Dante's gut, I gathered I hadn't. He grinned at me and winked. My heart swelled when he scooped me up into his arms.

"I love it when you big me up in front of my friends."

"I love it when you're just up me."

My eyes widened and I grabbed hold of the table to steady myself. "Star?"

I gawped at him. "Garth. You nearly hit me with a football!"

He chuckled with amazement and nodded. "I did. Only nearly though."

I reached out and placed my palm on his chest as tears filled my eyes. "I remember you."

"What the fuck!" Dante hissed as he snatched my hand away from Garth. I was so excited I didn't struggle with him.

"Dante!" I laughed. "I remember Garth. He threw a football at me at school." Dante stared at me, his eyes wide. "You were there too," I continued. "You scooped me up in your arms and kissed me." His stare grew into a huge smile, one that melted my insides.

"You remember?"

I nodded. "Just that piece but… but that means that I may be getting my memory back."

"That's brilliant, Star!" Malik gushed from the side of me. I nodded to him, his wide smile firing up another of my own.

"Will you sort out your fucking whore!" Dante suddenly shouted at Hunter, making us all jump.

She was staring at me again but this time her eyes were wide instead of narrow, her features still holding shock but it was as though my flashback had surprised her.

"Is there something wrong?" I asked her, growing angry at her rudeness.

Her eyes widened further before they shifted to Hunter. He marched across the room, seizing her in a tight grip. She lowered her face to the floor immediately, almost submissively.

"Okay," Malik interjected quickly. "I dunno about you but I'm thirsty." He smiled at us all then selected a bottle of whisky from the cupboard on the side and gathered up some glasses.

Passing the full glasses around, I frowned when the girls stood to one side of the room. They weren't spoken to, nor were they offered drinks. "You forgot your guests," I whispered to Malik, surprised by his bad manners.

He gave me a confused expression then lifted a brow. "Oh, they're not guests, Star."

"Dinner!" Dante exclaimed, leading me into another room off the one we were in.

A large table was catered for six diners. It was only then I noticed the other guest, a small man with slicked back hair. He gave me the creeps, the way his inquisitive gaze found mine. He tipped his head, his eyes narrow. A trickle slipped up my spine at the blatant coldness in his expression.

"Garth's boyfriend," Dante whispered in my ear when he caught my tension.

"Ohh."

Dante pulled out a chair for me, pushing it under me gradually as I sat. I studied each man as they sat. It didn't go unnoticed that I was the only female actually eating. Leaning into Dante when the men talked among themselves, he inclined towards me. "Are they prostitutes?"

His chest heaved as he tried to contain his humor. His mouth opened then closed again. Turning to me, he slipped his hand over my thigh, the silk of my dress bunching under his palm. "The girls are... I'm not quite sure how to put this." I frowned up at him, amazed at his loss of speech for the first time since getting to know him – again. "Playthings. Toys. Items of pleasure."

"Prostitutes," I restated.

"I suppose." He smiled down at me and ran his finger over my cheekbone, my heart purring under his tenderness. "The guys like to come over and... play."

"What?" I spluttered, the small mouthful of glazed prawn I'd just devoured spat back onto the table with an undignified slap. "Jesus holy Christ, Dante. I can't..."

"No! No, no," he placated. "We don't play."

My lungs decided they needed that bit of air they had just gushed out and I started to choke on the rapid intake of oxygen. The men halted their conversation and looked at me. "Went down the wrong way," Dante excused for me as he tapped my back.

They smiled then carried on with their conversation, apart from Malik who I caught sneakily watching us.

"Well why do they come here to...play?" I had an awful feeling I wouldn't like where this was going.

"Because you have a fetish, voyeurism. Actually, you prefer to be the one being watched. But I was building up to that until you forced my hand in the game you insisted on us playing. Before that we just watched them play." His statement was so casual I just nodded. Then realization hit me and I gawped at him.

"We... what? We... we watch?"

He shrugged, biting into his own food. My heart plummeted. "It's what you like, Star."

"What? No. No, I can honestly tell you it's *not* what I like."

He sighed as though I was boring him. "Will you calm down? You're starting to embarrass me."

I scoffed, amazement and disbelief making me stare. "I'm so sorry. To be quite honest, I *am* embarrassed! How can we do this? I don't want to do this!" My chair screeched as I shot upright and glared at him. "You know what, I can't do this." I was fuming. How dare he put me in this situation? Embarrassment was an understatement.

I felt every single pair of eyes on me as I turned away. They wanted to play; well they could play without me, that was for certain.

CHAPTER 22

PERFORM

Dante

MY TEETH VIBRATED WITH THE fury that swelled inside. How dare she humiliate me like that! All eyes in the room were now on me, Hunter's smirk and Malik's tipped eyebrow proof that they were laughing at me inside. "Engagement not running as smoothly as you'd have liked, Troy?" Hunter snorted.

Throwing my napkin on the table, I turned my lips upwards into a cruel sneer. "Her feistiness is what makes me hard, Hunter. Excuse me while I tend to the *problem*."

They all stared at me. Yeah, fuck them all.

The door bashed against the wall when I punched it open. My footing stuttered to a stop when I witnessed Hunter's slut with her hand on Star's arm, holding her in position while she spoke feverishly to her.

"Please. Even on a napkin, hell, my boob, thigh anywhere will do..."

Star stared at her in bewilderment. "I..."

"You have no idea how fucking shocked I was to see you. I mean...

you, of all people I never expected to be here …although Mr Troy … It makes sense. I'm new to… Hunter but he said his friend, the big guy with the scar, liked them young and needed a good night so he was going to bring me. I had no idea."

"I think you have the wrong…."

"But there you were," the stupid blonde bitch gushed. "Like I'd walked into wonderland." Her eyes roved the room frantically. "Damn, I don't think I have a pen! Fuck." She turned back to Star. "Do you? I bet you carry sharpies in your cleavage don't you, for moments like this."

Star's face was comical, her eyes as wide as her gaping mouth but this was far from funny. "Sharpie?"

The whore nodded. "Yeah, I bet you have a Cartier pen, what with you being all sophisticated and all that."

Jesus fucking hell!

"What are you doing?" I barked. Both her and Star jumped, spinning in my direction. Star's fury from earlier had disappeared, her face now showing her amazement at what was occurring.

The bitch's mouth dropped open again and she pointed one of her long talons at me. "He didn't tell me you'd be here and that she would be too!"

Christ. I glared at her until she cowered, her little feet moving backwards. She had a right to be scared. I was fucking furious.

"How dare you come into *my* house and behave like a crazy ass freak on crack! How – fucking – dare – you!"

Her eyes widened further, the color draining from her face. Hunter appeared through the door. "Get her out of here!"

He rolled his eyes and turned to his date. "Fucking hell, you stupid bitch. I told you to leave it."

I didn't wait for any more of his excuses. Grabbing hold of Star's hand I pulled her across the room and through the house, ending our swift escape in my office.

"What the hell was that all about?" She was still stunned, her eyes still wide and full of alarm.

I walked over to her slowly, the flow of anger inside me making it dangerous for her, but she needed to be taught a lesson after her behavior in front of my friends. "A crazy fan."

"What? A fan? Of who?"

"Of you, of course."

Her foot slid backwards slightly when she witnessed my struggle, my temper simmering on the surface. Unknotting my tie I slid it off and grabbed the high-backed chair from the corner of the room, positioning it in the middle of the floor facing the three screens that adorned the back wall.

"Me?" she spluttered.

"Mmm." I nodded as I took her hand and led her over to the chair, my eyes fixed on hers, refusing her any denial in following my silent order. I maneuvered her until she sat, the excitement in my gut bubbling furiously at the lesson I was about to teach my feisty little woman. "You're a renowned artist, Star. Your paintings are displayed worldwide. They decorate the most influential galleries."

"Really?" She looked up at me with wide, disbelieving eyes. I cupped her cheek, the softness to her chin calming the rage inside me slightly.

"Why so shocked? You never trusted in your talent, Star; no matter how much I told you how amazing it was."

"Well." She shrugged, not noticing the pull of her hands behind the chair as I ventured around the back of her. "It's me, isn't it? I'm just… me."

She flinched and frowned over her shoulder when she finally realized she was secured tightly to a wooden chair in the middle of my office. "Dante? What are you doing?" She struggled with her restraints, her eyes scared and her heart galloping beneath her breastbone.

"I'm showing you how *we* like to play, Belle."

She stilled when I pressed a button and the screens blinked to life, each one displaying a different angle in the lounge where our guests were situated. I growled when I spotted Hunter and his slut. The asshole hadn't heeded my order and left but I wasn't about to go back in there now, I had things right in front of me to deal with first.

"Oh my God," she squeaked when her eyes landed on the performance playing out just for us. My heart rate quickened, my pulse charging blood into my cock, my eyes feasting on the orgy that was happening right in my house.

I chuckled and settled myself on the sofa in front of Star, and to the left of the screens.

She was transfixed on what was taking place. Disgust was written all over her face but she couldn't quite gain the command to remove her gaze from it.

"Quite something isn't it?"

Her eyes flicked my way, shock and amazement were evident but something else flickered in her expression. I knew it would find its way. I knew her better than she thought.

Leaning forward and resting my elbows on my thighs, I licked my lips, causing her eyes to drop to watch. She squirmed slightly. I was astounded arousal had found her so quickly. "You see how both Malik and Hunter fill that girl? How cute her ass looks with Hunter's cock buried deep inside. Would you like that, Star? My cock sliding in and out, in and out of your ass slowly and so fucking deeply?"

She coughed, her eyes glancing back at the screens then back to me. Her breathing had deepened, her soft pink lips parted to accommodate her rapid pants. "And look. See how Garth glides his dick between Ben's lips. Two men fucking, there's something quite erotic about that."

Her throat bobbed as her ass slid against the seat of the chair. I smiled when the scent of her arousal filled my senses. "Would you like to watch me being fucked by a man, Star? Watch your fiancé get pummeled in the ass?" That wasn't going to happen but my dirty little slut loved to hear me talk dirty to her.

"Oh God, Dante. Stop." Her breathy request had me lowering my zip and pulling out my dick, the scorch of heat on my rigid shaft almost burning my hand when I wrapped my fist around myself. Her eyes dropped to watch me masturbate, need firing in her eyes as her tongue stroked her bottom lip.

"Eyes on the screen, baby."

She pulled at her bindings but the knot was tight, rejecting her attempts. Her legs parted slightly, the slit in her dress allowing for it. Stroking myself harder I turned my eyes back to the party.

Star released a small moan when she also watched the recital. "Oh, shit."

"Oh, how fucking beautiful." One of the screens exhibited a closer view than the rest, showing Hunter's whore's tongue lap at the other girl's pussy, the torture of her clit making cum seep from the end of my dick and dribble down my shaft. I started to stroke faster, needing release quickly.

"Look at that, Star. The worship of a woman's cunt by another woman. Can you imagine her tongue inside your hot little pussy, driving pleasure through you while my cock fills your perfect ass?"

"Dante." She moaned my name and opened her thighs further, showing me the swollen lips of her pink bald pussy while the string of her thong hid the most delicious part from me, it's tease an exquisite torture. "Please."

"There is something so sexy about looking, but not touching. Right, baby? The imagination fed by what it sees, beckoning scintillating thoughts that heat the blood and awaken your body." I pumped my cock harder. "I get why you want to be watched. Seeing sexual desire reflected in the eyes of the voyeur is a powerful thing."

I smiled, relishing in her hunger. She licked her lips again as she watched me jerk off, my fist tight, my strokes hard and fast. My balls tightened, my spine tingled, my thighs clenched. I shot upright and took the single step needed to reach her. She tilted her face up to me, her eyes both pleading and hoping.

"Open your mouth. Take what I give you."

She didn't argue. Her lips parted, a small groan releasing with the action. Sprays of cum shot over her face, a shower of cream surging from me to her as her tongue came out to catch each drop. Fuck, she looked stunning as she wore me, her eyes adoring what I gave her, her little pink tongue licking my seed off her lips, devouring me.

Every single muscle in my body clenched, pulling my back into an arc as I squeezed every drop out, admiring it drip over her flushed pink skin.

She stared up at me, waiting, anticipating. I ran my thumb over a bead of cum that sat on her cheek then pushed it into her mouth, she wrapped her tongue around it, eager for more. "Greed is a selfish thing, Belle."

She frowned at me, her gaze dropping to watch me tuck myself back in my pants. Her gawp on me was amusing when I reached behind her and tapped her wrists. "I'm leaving these so you don't touch yourself." I smirked before I walked to the door and opened it.

"But…" she stuttered. I turned to her and quirked an eyebrow in question. "You can't just… do that then leave me."

I chuckled at her. "Why? You don't like to play, do you Star?"

I left her with that statement. Next time she wouldn't be so fucking quick to judge.

CHAPTER 23

VOYEUR

Star

HE REALLY LEFT ME THERE. I awaited his footsteps, for the door to open and him to tell me he was joking, but nothing. I sat and watched our dinner guest enjoy dessert from the toys they brought with them. My eyes scanned the screens and my breath stole. Dante walked into the room where everyone was fucking some part of everyone else. He was saying something to Hunter, his face pinched in aggravation. He then walked over to the crazy fan girl, gripping a fist full of her hair and dragging her from the room. My heart was being swallowed by the empty hole growing in my stomach. I didn't care who I was before this but I couldn't bear if he touched another woman and expected me to be okay with that. Fuck no!

I grappled at the restraints but the bastard was an expert at tying knots. Tears began to build until movement caught my attention on the outdoor porch monitor. Dante stood over the girl who was naked on her knees in front of him. Pointing his finger in her face he appeared to berate her. Then he walked in and closed the door leaving her sitting on our porch naked.

Two freaking hours I sat there. I had watched everyone, including Dante, come. Fan girl sat on the porch without moving until Hunter finished up and took her away with him. Everyone had left and I was frustrated, irritated and my arms ached. My eyes grew tired. I just wanted a hot soak to loosen the tight muscles in my shoulder, and then crawl in bed.

The door swung open, making me sit up from the slouch I had found myself in. Malik entered the room, he looked startled to see me tied to a chair, and after seeing him naked and thrusting into every orifice on his plaything's body I couldn't look him in the eye.

We were both still in the room which seemed to grow smaller by the minute. I noticed his head turn to the monitors in front of me. A weird groaning noise came from him but I still couldn't bring myself to look up at him.

"Star, I'm sorry you had to see me like that."

Okay, so not what I was expecting. I was hoping he would just grab what he came for, be a Gent and untie me then leave without either of us speaking. I swallowed down my discomfort and embarrassment and shrugged. "Not like I haven't seen it all before, apparently." My tone lacked the conviction I intended to portray. He winced and shuffled from one foot to the other. "Can you untie me?"

He backed up like I had asked him to commit a murder. "Oh, I can't do that."

I cut him off. "Malik, seriously?"

He closed his eyes. I waited for a few silent seconds and then he exhaled, coming towards me. He freed me, rubbing my sore wrists as he shook his head. I didn't need him judging me or Dante. Yeah, it was an asshole move but this was who we were and Malik of all people should have known that.

Standing and pulling my dress into place, I offered him a small smile before leaving him standing there.

For some reason I found myself creeping through the house and up the stairs. I felt like I had sneaked out of the naughty cupboard my mom used to lock me in when I was a kid.

Air rushed into my lungs from my quick inhale as I slammed to a halt, my eyes widening at the internal revelation. I remembered just like that. Not images, only knowledge of a truth. Oh God, to think of my mom gave me an eerie feeling. We didn't get on, she was horrible. I couldn't place solid memories but I knew we had a turbulent relationship.

I wanted to rush and tell Dante but I felt apprehensive. Would he be pissed that Malik had released me? Maybe I should claim that I'd managed to free myself.

"Why are you standing on the stairs?"

I squeaked a little at the sound of his voice. I couldn't determine his mood. "I, I uhh…"

Rolling his eyes he glued me to the spot with an icy glare. "Stop fucking stuttering! Answer me!"

Okay, his mood was sour.

How dare he act this shitty towards me? I was the one going numb in his office while he was doing God knows what! "I was on my way to bed and then I remembered something about my mom."

He came down the few steps separating us. "What was it?" Shaking off the daunting feeling I had when I thought of her, I shook my head and lifted a shoulder in a defeated shrug. No one wanted to admit their parent was hostile. His caress was gentle as he reached for my hand, the pad of his thumb stroking over my wrist. "Your mother was a selfish old bitch! Her death was a blessing."

Oh God, she was dead? I didn't know how to respond or how to feel. I didn't feel anything really, only a little emptier inside.

I let him lead me to our bedroom. He stripped me from my dress and guided me to the bathroom. He freed himself from his clothes and pulled me into the shower, turning it on. I let him satisfy my body. I was strung too tight. I combusted into an intense orgasm as soon as his lips closed over the tight bundle of nerves just inside the folds of my pussy. He was an expert with his tongue; his hands knew every inch of my body from the years of exploring it. His cock fit me to perfection, grazing the front wall where my delicious g-spot awaited him. Every lap of his tongue, slide of his hand, stroke of his cock was precise and designed to bring me to my knees.

I was left in a sated mess as he tucked me under the sheets after our shower. I wasn't completely asleep when he left the room.

CHAPTER 24

DREAMS

Star

KISSES BEGAN AT MY ANKLES, urging me from my slumber as they travelled up my calves and thighs, inhaling over my mound then up to my navel. "Mmm, I'm so in love with you, baby. I can't wait for you to own my name."

His body became completely flush with mine, his eyes looking down into mine adoringly. Wow, the intensity of his love shone so bright down on me. "I want to be inside you so bad but this tattoo needs to heal," he whined. My eyes widened. "I can still taste you though." He grinned nuzzling into my neck.

He seemed so carefree. Where was the Dante from last night? "Mmm, what's that smell?"

His head lifted, a cinnamon aroma filling the air. "Room service. You ordered me pancakes. I can't stand the food on set. I need to be there in an hour so ssh and let me enjoy my first breakfast before my pancakes." He disappeared under the sheet covering our bodies.

"What?"

"I said Matilda made you breakfast."

My eyes shot open at the sound of Dante's voice booming across the room. It was a dream? No - a memory. Sitting up way too fast I called out, halting Dante's departure from the room. "Do you have any other tattoos?"

His icy glare from last night was back as he turned to me and ate up the distance between us, coming to stand at the foot of the bed. "No, why?"

It was so real but maybe it could have been a dream. Lying back down, I shook my head. "Just a dream." He stood in silence, looking down on me. "Can we go somewhere?" I asked into the room without looking at him. "I know we're on an island but Hunter and the others came here so we must be close to land right?"

I felt his anger, like a shadow coating the bed, seeping closer to snare me in its darkness. "I have work!"

"Can I go then?" I shouldn't have had to ask permission but I had no clue where to begin getting off the island.

"I don't want you out without me. You have no memories."

I needed space, the thought of being trapped there was making me claustrophobic, like an itch under my skin making me jittery and frustrated.

"What about work? Don't they miss me?"

"You have a studio at the back of the house."

I sat up. "Really?"

A small tilt to the side of his mouth eased some of the anger from his features. "Yes. Would you like me to show you after breakfast?"

What he said earlier registered. "Wait, who's Matilda?"

"She's my cook and maid and… well everything." Huh!

I threw on some jeans and a loose fitting tee and made my way to breakfast. The table was filled with a buffet of food and no one eating. I walked into the kitchen to find Dante holding a paper and drinking what I assumed was coffee. Malik was beside him, whispering in his ear. Both sets of eyes came to stop on me. I awkwardly raised a hand with a weird wave. Dante arched a brow and Malik averted his gaze. It was then I noticed a cast on his hand. Walking over to him with my mouth open, I reached for his arm, to be stopped by Dante's hand capturing mine. "What are you doing?" he questioned.

"What happened?"

Malik looked to the floor instead of at me when he replied. I was all the more aware of his need to hide from me, his action driving my curiosity higher. "I had an accident last night, it's nothing. The doctor came straight out and fixed it."

"It's in a cast," I told him like he didn't know

"It's just a fracture, Star. He's a big boy, it will remind him to be more careful when handling things he shouldn't be." Malik left the room with Dante's eyes following his retreat.

"Is there something I should know?" I asked, feeling somehow responsible. Malik wouldn't look at me, and after he untied me last night, I couldn't help the nervous ball of energy that lived as a constant in my stomach from warning me that Dante no doubt did this. But would he be that brutal? Flashbacks suddenly assaulted me of him telling me he sorted Theo and that he was gone for good. My breathing picked up pace as the unease settled in the atmosphere around us.

"You only need to know what I tell you! Malik is not your concern and in future you'll do well to remember who you belong to! If I wanted you untied I would have done it myself."

The rush of air from my lungs expelled from me in a gust. Goosebumps laced every inch of my skin. I stared at him, my mouth as wide as my eyes. "You broke his fucking hand, Dante!"

He moved so quick it was almost inhuman, grasping a fistful of my hair just like he did to the fan skank last night. "You belong to me! He had no right untying you and he knows it. He only did it because you made him, so *YOU* broke his hand." He released me with a shove.

Tears were already on my cheeks, the sting from his grasp setting fire to my scalp. The empty feeling inside me grew, swallowing more of me. Screw him! What a crazy fuck. Who breaks their friend's hand?

Rushing to our room, I went straight to the closet and began packing a bag. Twenty minutes later I was out the front door. I ignored his presence behind me and ran. There was a dock, I would sit and wait for someone to come by and then I would ask them for a lift to shore.

"What are you doing?"

I wouldn't answer him; my voice would only waver from my tears and the lump clogging my throat.

"Fine, Star. Have it your way." His footfalls faded as he left me.

My tears washed away like the tide. The ripples of the water lapping at the wooden platform relaxed me. I hadn't realized how tense I was until my muscles uncoiled. The vast amounts of water reminded me of my life. On the surface there was nothing. A bare slate of blue, but underneath there was life, a whole world that couldn't be seen. I wanted so bad to break through the surface of my memories to the world underneath but there was only ripples of who I was teasing the surface.

An hour later I was still there and the sun was beginning to redden my skin. Why did it always seem like I was left waiting? I heard movements behind me and then the buzzing, almost growling sound swooshing over the water. A speed boat. An older woman walked towards me from the house, her greying hair piled high on her head. She was tiny, well under five foot. She didn't acknowledge me. What the hell? She walked right past me like I was invisible.

The boat pulled to a stop, a young guy driving, the only passenger. His eyes nearly fell from his head when he saw me standing there. I checked behind me to make sure it was definitely me he was gaping at. Screw it. I would flirt a little to get a lift. "Hey." I smiled, picking up my bag. "Can you take me with you?" His mouth actually fell open. The woman I assumed was Matilda shook her head and waved her finger then spoke in a different language to the boy. He then shook his head and appeared scared, his face a tad paler and his eyes staring at me. What the actual hell?

I stormed back up towards the house and found Dante standing against the doorframe, arms crossed, face void of reaction.

"What's going on, Dante? Why didn't they take me?"

He snatched the bag from my shoulder, throwing it inside the house. "Because you belong to me! It's not their place to take you anywhere. Why won't you stop being difficult and learn your place!" My mouth fell open in an O. Was he serious?

"Did you really kill Theo?" I knew I'd caught him off guard, and in truth I didn't give a shit about that disgusting little worm but I needed to know who I was letting in my body. Did the other me know he was capable of such brutality?

Ah crap! He was pissed and I found myself suddenly backing up from his approaching fury. He crowded my entire frame with his, engulfing me in his sea of loathing. "That cunt got what he deserved. How dare you bring up his name to me!"

How dare I? I was that 'cunt's' victim, not him. "Fuck you!" I spat and regretted it as soon as it left my mouth. His hand shot out around my throat.

"Fine with me."

I found myself over his shoulder again, being carried through the house. Déjà vu once again.

We passed Malik, whose eyebrows reached his hairline when he saw me clawing at Dante's back while screaming for him to put me down. "What's going on?" he asked. Dante stopped his fast pace, turning on Malik.

"You, follow me!" he commanded, and like a freaking puppy, Malik fell in step behind him, looking down at my bobbing head.

"You both need to fucking learn this lesson. Sit."

Malik took the seat at the head of the table still littered with plates of untouched food. It looked amazing and reminded me how hungry I was. With a swipe of his arm, Dante knocked everything onto the floor with a startling crash, making both me and Malik jump. Fear trickled into my veins. I had awoken a beast.

"You need to accept your fate. This is your life, Star. You belong here with me. You know it and yet you keep fighting it. Why?" He didn't expect an answer. "I gave up so fucking much for you. Done shit I'm not proud of, and this is what I get - a fucking brat who refuses to remember her love for me."

How did he manage to make me feel so angry at him in one breath, only to feel guilty and ashamed of my behavior in the next? *I'm sorry* was on the tip of my tongue. Even though my brain told me he was in the wrong, his instability proof of it, my heart still told me I made him this way. I had made him go through with that stupid fantasy and now we… we were broken. He had a fiancée, a woman who loved him and now he had this shell, this carcass of confusion.

Placing me on the table, he yanked my jeans from my body, making me screech in surprise. "You both crossed lines. You both broke rules. You both need to remember who owns who!"

What the fuck did that mean? And how was taking my jeans off going to do that, and more to the point, what was I? A freaking object?

Pure rage and fire lit his eyes; it was like looking at the sun. I had to turn away. He flipped me with ease onto my stomach, pulling my legs over the edge of the opposite end to where Malik was seated. My feet touched the floor, my torso flush with the table top. Kicking my feet apart, my breath hitched. I tried to raise myself up but his heavy hand came down between my shoulder blades, forcing me back down. No way was he going to do what I thought he was.

"Hold her arms," he demanded. A heavy hand came down on my wrists, pulling them together and stretching my arms out in front of me above my head. Malik was almost replicating my position on the other side of me. His torso against the table, his palm wrapped around my wrists. I felt a tugging on my ankle and then weighty material wrapped around it, tying me to the table leg. It was my jeans. A tug between my legs, a rip shattering the silence, and then my other ankle being tied with the panties he tore from me. I couldn't look at the confliction in Malik's face; there was lust in his eyes and I knew the table hid his erection. I turned my face, laying my wet cheek from the fall of my tears against the cool wood of the table.

"I don't think so, Belle," Dante spat. I heard him stripping, the wisp of his belt and the sharp snap of his zip lowering then the thud of his slacks hitting the floor. The leather of his belt came over my face to rest against my throat forcing my head up to look straight into Malik's eyes. The belt tightened as Dante tugged on it like reins on a horse. He gave me no foreplay, no warning. His cock nudged at my opening and then thrust straight into my body. Malik's eyes flashed when I was jolted forward towards him. "Your dirty little pussy was made for my hard cock, Star. Even when you deny it you can't deny the wetness coating my cock right now." *Thrust.* "Who owns you?" *Thrust.*

Fuck him! I wasn't going to answer. I could barely breathe from the leather belt cutting into my windpipe. My tears fell harder, their torrent stinging my lip where I had bit into it and distorting the image of Malik's lust. The bastard. My body was the biggest bastard in the room because it answered everything Dante was giving it. My core tightened and pulsed, the heat rushing through me in waves. My nipples were hard, pushing against the fabric of my bra and tee. "Who owns you, Star? Use your words." The condescending asshole.

"Fuck you!" I growled.

His thrusts became harder, pushing me to the brink. "Oh, you want to fuck me?" The belt left my throat in a slice sure to leave a mark. It burned. He must have communicated with his eyes to Malik because my hands were freed from his tight hold. Sweat from his palm left a wet sticky layer there. Gross!

Dante's cock slipped from me, my mouth mewed from his loss making me cringe at my own need for him. I was such a cock whore. "Aww, my little slut missing me already yet refuses to admit I own her."

A chair scraped behind me then I was pulled upright. His hard cock re-entered me, making me moan. His teeth nipped at my ear and neck before sinking into my shoulder, making me wince and groan at the same time. Lowering us down, he sat on a chair with me on his lap. His belt wrapped around my wrists this time and then he looped them over his head to rest around his neck. Hot palms splayed against my inner thighs pushing them open to bare me to the cool air and Malik's greedy eyes. "Look how pink and perfect she is. My filthy girl." I couldn't stop my hips from moving, grinding down on him in quest of the release I knew he could bring me. Everything else disappeared. It was just me and the pleasure seeking. His thumb circled my exposed clit, his words lifting me into a state of euphoria.

"Look how I make her juices leak from her; how I make her pussy squeeze my big thick cock. Strangle my dick, Star. Fuck me my beautiful, Belle. Make me fill you up."

That was it; I screamed my release, my inner walls demanding his. The groans echoed all around, his throbbing cock pulsing his release into me. Hot ribbons of cum flooded me and leaked from me when he lifted my hips to slip free from me. His fingers replaced his cock, gathering his cum and rubbing it all over every inch of my pussy. "Who do you belong to?" he whispered.

"You," I panted my response.

"Who does she belong to?"

"You," Malik replied, reminding me of his presence.

I closed my eyes and waited until I heard their footsteps fade before I sank to the floor and sobbed into my hands.

CHAPTER 25

DECEPTION

Star

I REMAINED THERE FOR A long time, my unblinking eyes fixed on a random point on the wall. My fingers stroked over my sore neck, the tender skin under my touch shriveling back at the contact.

I wasn't sure what the hell had just happened. My thoughts wouldn't sort themselves out, the jumbled mass of rapid fire self-questioning giving me a headache. I knew whatever I thought, or Dante thought for that matter, that what had transpired was far from okay. It was wrong, very wrong. He was like this addiction, the pleasure he gave me overruling all the depravity he dished out, the drug he fed me outweighing the corruption made to get the high.

Life or relationships shouldn't be like that. Although I wasn't aware of what my life entailed, I knew deep down that this wasn't what I wanted; however breaking away was easier said than done.

The high from my intense orgasm contradicted the raw pain on my neck... and in my heart. Although dominance was sometimes a sexual stimulant, Dante had taken that a step further, a step too far. The humiliation caused my stomach to twist over the fact that Malik had watched, disgust rolling over me.

I forced myself up from the floor, grabbing my jeans and redressing as I tried desperately to shut off the turmoil in my head.

I wandered the house aimlessly, my feet scuffing the floor in my desolation. Although the house was huge, I had never felt more isolated. Its many walls crushed my spirit, its mass of rooms doing nothing to stop the lonely ache inside me.

I ended my walk when I discovered an open door at the end of a long hallway I hadn't come across before. Pushing it ajar I stared at the huge open space. A large window filled the whole of one wall, allowing so much natural light in that it was almost as if heaven greeted me. Three easels of different sizes were stood empty, various palettes leaning against the legs. Paints filled several shelves, an array of colors, tubes, pots, brushes and bottles kitting out the room for when I felt ready to return to something I apparently not only loved, but was good at.

My feet took me further in, my eyes still scanning every corner. A sink was situated behind the door, towels and aprons hung from hooks above. But I bypassed those and came to stand in front of a gigantic canvas. The scene took my breath. It was the house here, painted from an angle which suggested the front garden. Peering at it closer, I saw my name scrawled in the bottom right-hand corner. I stood in awe, looking at what my fingers created, the soft brush strokes apparently painted by me sweeping the watercolor elegantly and expertly.

I was amazed by my skill, yet something didn't sit right. I couldn't place my finger on what was bugging me as I stared restlessly around the studio, trying desperately to find what didn't make sense.

Shrugging it off, I selected a brush from one of the pots and picked up a tube of blue acrylic paint, squeezing a small amount onto a palette. Even the equipment felt *wrong* but I put it down to my lack of memories.

Pulling an easel over to the window, I settled myself in front of it and dipped the brush into the paint then lifted it to the canvas. I wasn't sure what I expected but nothing came, not even an image in my head to start with.

Swallowing back the annoyance, I diverted my gaze through the window trying to find a subject I could paint. A huge tree caught my attention, pink blossom covering its branches and the surrounding grass beneath it with a rustic iron bench situated to one side. Okay, that should be quite pretty to recreate.

I ventured back over to the shelf, picking a selection of assorted colors, expelling a tiny amount of each onto the palette with the original blue. White, green, red, yellow and blue now decorated the clean white plastic. I blinked again, angry at what was troubling me.

"Damn it, Star. Think."

Inhaling deeply, I dipped the brush into the red, collecting a small amount before swirling it into the mixing compartment. Taking a measure of white I mixed it with the red. The pink I produced was a little gaudy so I mixed in a little more white. My gaze kept flicking to the blossom as I tried to form the exact color but it wasn't working, the shade of pink either too harsh or too pale.

"God damn it, it can't be that hard."

Picking another brush I went to mix a brown. What were the colors I needed again? How did you create a brown, was it red and blue? Yellow, blue and green?

I couldn't do anything; my memories were like a disability, holding me back from myself and my abilities.

I spun round, flinging the palette across the room. Paint sprayed across the floor then splattered the wall where it crashed into it, a rainbow the only thing I could actually create. I stared at the mess, the wall now my canvas as a variety of color spread out in lines and splodges.

I narrowed my eyes and slowly looked around. Nothing. There was no other mess in the room. And that was the problem. I tipped my head and studied the wooden floor. Nothing. My gaze lifted to the other three walls. Nothing.

I frowned, reaching for the supply of paintbrushes. All clean and brand new. Several pristine white palettes were piled up beside brand new tubes of paint, their seals still intact when I unscrewed numerous ones to check. I yanked an apron from a hook; it was still creased from where it had obviously been sat in its packaging. The sink was steel, its glare almost blinding.

"Holy shit!"

If this was my studio where I created my art, including the painting in the corner with my signature scribbled on it why was everything so new?

My mouth dried as my heartbeat sped up. I dropped into a chair that sat beside a wooden table and lifted a hand to my mouth as though it would stop the need to vomit. Why? Why lie to me? He had to be lying, there was no way this was a used studio. Even if it had been cleaned there would be old brushes and pallets, there would be paint rags. Right?

The painting of the house mocked me. Did I paint that? I looked down at my name in the corner of the painting, *Star Numan.*

It was definitely my name. Grabbing some paper and a pencil, I signed my name, Star Numan, according to the autograph on the picture.

The pencil hovered over the paper, even my signature caused my brain difficulty but I forced myself.

Star Numan.

Star Numan

Star Numan.

Why was it so hard to find the same scrawl as the one I obviously always used? I forced myself harder, my eyes glued to the autograph on the painting as I tried to recreate an autograph I would have written frequently. My eyes narrowed as I stared harder and let the pen flow, refusing to watch myself write, hoping it came more naturally. A smile lifted my lips when I finally felt the pencil flow easily, the deep sweep of my hand moving fluently. However when I dropped my gaze to the paper, the floor shifted under me.

Star Numan

Star Numan

Star Avery

Faye Avery

Faye Avery

Faye Avery

Faye Avery

The chair screeched across the floor when I shot upright, the pounding in my chest painful and suffocating. What the fuck? Who the hell was Faye Avery? My head shook from side to side as my mind started to buzz.

"Faye!" I turned to see Jennifer waving as she ran towards me. "Where have you been?"

I shrugged, heat climbing up my face. "I...uhh..."

*"Faye Avery! You've been with **him** again, haven't you?"*

The shame generated a tear which dribbled down my face as I shook my head at my best friend. "Jen... I... Oh shit, what the hell am I gonna do?"

Her brow creased. "Babe?"

"I... I can't do this. I'm not sure it's what I want. Hell, I don't even know what Dante wants apart from the need to control me. But..." The floor seemed to shift beneath me and I swayed. Jennifer grabbed my hands and directed me onto the university steps. "Faye, talk to me. What is it?"

"He... I...."

"Star?" My body shook when Dante's voice pulled me from the memory. I stared at him, his face feeling both foreign and familiar. "Are you okay?"

I closed my mouth, running my tongue over my teeth to coat them when they stuck to my lips. Nodding, I smiled weakly up at him. "Yeah." He frowned at the tremble in my voice. "I just went a bit dizzy."

He studied me for a moment. "Are you..." He grumbled when his phone rang in his pocket. He pulled it out and answered, telling the caller to hold on before he turned back to me. "I have to go, baby. Are you sure you're okay?"

I nodded, forcing a smile. I was well aware of the piece of paper on the table, my signature all over it. I wasn't sure if I could deal with his reasons or excuses yet, and his wrath if I did question him was causing the tremble in my lip. He held the back of his hand to my forehead but shrugged, "You don't have a temperature."

"Honestly, Dante, I'm fine."

He looked around the room as if finally realizing where we were and I quickly covered the paper with a fresh piece to hide it. "Oh," he said, before turning back to me. "Have you managed to do much?"

I swallowed to remove the restriction in my throat. "No, to be honest I'm struggling."

He gave me a sad smile then leaned into me, his soft lips kissing my forehead. "It'll come, baby. Give it time."

I nodded in return. He seemed so sincere, but I hadn't imagined the evidence this room was not a studio where I'd worked, I knew it. "Yeah."

He sighed then held up his phone, reminding me he had to go.

"I'm okay, better now. Go."

He nodded and walked away but then paused near the door and turned back to me. "Listen, I'm sorry… about earlier." I didn't answer him, I couldn't and if I was being honest with myself about how wrong it was then I needed to be as honest with him because there was no way I ever wanted a replay of what transpired earlier.

I released the breath I was holding trying to cover my anxious state by looking down at my feet instead of directly at him.

"I… I don't like that side of you, Dante. You scare me." It was the truth and since seeing this room and writing a completely different name to the one he and everyone used for me, that couldn't have been truer.

"Mmm." He nodded as if agreeing with me, stunning me. "I have to sort something but go put on a dress and meet me in the hallway in about an hour."

I stared at him with a frown. "Why?"

"I think it's about time I took you on a date."

I couldn't stop my eyes from widening. "You mean… on land?"

He chuckled, transforming his usual stern expression into light-hearted beauty. "Well, I have many things to cater for my personal side in the house but a restaurant is not one of them. So yes, we'll be dining on the mainland tonight."

I couldn't contain all the emotions bubbling in my gut, relief to actually be leaving the house and excitement at actually being around other people. Maybe I could slip away, find somewhere to stay for a while until I could find out all the things not making sense.

I was trembling and annoyed with myself for it. He would notice my behavior and assume I was really sick, changing his mind about taking me. I schooled my meltdown. Inhaling a calming breath, I slipped a façade into place. "Thank you," I said with a fake grin, one I imitated well according to his answering smile back at me, albeit soft.

His steps reduced the space between us, his fingers gently running across my lips. "You have such a beautiful smile."

My heart swelled and then deflated with his genuine tenderness. I was so confused by everything. My emotions were shredded, I felt like just when I grasped onto something it was ripped from me to mock me, taunt me. Who was Star? Who was Faye? Who was Dante?

"That's because you put it there." I tried not to flinch at my own lies.

Maybe I was seeing too much into my name, maybe I used a pen name of sorts and everyone called me by that? My mind was trying to find a reasonable explanation but my heart pounding in my chest was telling me my instincts were correct… None of this was normal.

I needed to look for my passport or bank statements to confirm my identity before asking Dante to explain himself. I needed proof so he couldn't feed me another story or deny my claims. He had a way of making me forget my questions. Forget the wrong in everything happening around me, to me. He made me feel responsible for taking away his apparently kinky and totally in love fiancé. I didn't want to question his motives without proof and ruin the chance of him not taking me inland.

"Then I must remember to make you smile more often."

His voice brought me out of my musings. He was studying my face. I nodded, biting my lip seductively to cover the doubt in my eyes as I pushed him towards the door. "Go, hurry with what you need to do. I'll be waiting."

He laughed, shaking his head at my eagerness before he turned and pulled the door to behind him.

I couldn't breathe! I collapsed to the ground dragging air into my lungs. I startled when a shrill rang out into the room. Scanning the walls and surfaces for the ringing phone, I located a sleek black handset on the far wall.

"Hello?" I answered warily.

"Don't get lost in any work Belle, you need to get ready!" The phone dial echoed down the line. That was it?

Oh god I was holding a phone… but who could I call?

Holding the phone I stared at the digits before my thumb worked over the keypad from memory, my eyes widening at the surprising recollection of numbers. Ringing sounded through the ear piece. My mouth dropped open, my ragged breathing almost dulling out the sound. Adrenaline pumped my heart harder.

Click

"Who's this?"

Gasping I dropped the receiver. It was Dante. He sounded upset. I scrambled to pick it up.

"I'm sorry… I'm getting ready now."

His intake of breath seized my heart. I quickly ended the call. I ran from the room towards our bedroom to get ready, my strides as fast as my heart beat.

Applying another coat of lipstick I studied the finished me in the mirror and practiced my smile. I hoped it would convince Dante.

My mind filtered back to earlier and the discovery of my real name. "Shit!" I hissed when I realized I'd left the paper on the table for him to find.

Rushing back to the studio, I snatched it up and tore it into tiny long strips, making it indecipherable, then went to drop the pieces into the bin in front of the window.

A movement outside caught my attention. A small brick building sat at the very back of the garden. It was virtually covered in ivy which was the reason I hadn't spotted it earlier.

My stomach tightened when Dante stepped out with the doctor. Shit, what was her name? She was talking to Dante, her mouth moving rapidly as he buttoned up his shirt. She said something to him and he threw his head back and laughed. Dante never laughed; unless he just didn't laugh around me. Even from far away I saw the lust in her eyes. She bit her lip and reached up to straighten his collar, rubbing her hand down the planes of his chest and abs. Tears sprung to my eyes but I blinked them back. Dante nodded at her then turned and locked the door, slipping the key into his pocket as the doctor slid her hand up and down his arm.

I winced when my teeth sank so far into my bottom lip I could taste the copper tang of my blood. He nodded again, saying something to her before she turned and walked towards the driveway as Dante ventured up the garden towards the house.

My heart skipped when her head turned up, her gaze colliding briefly with mine. Her step faltered for a second but then she stopped. I watched in mortification as she slipped something out of her pocket; panties. She stood right there for me to see as she slipped them up her legs back into place. What a skanky whore! She told me we were friends.

I screwed my eyes shut and turned away from the window before he spotted me. It was obvious what they had been doing. I didn't like her when I first met her, and the bitch had claimed to be my friend. My vision blurred as my blood roared through my veins in fury. My fists clenched by my sides as my jaw tightened. I was so damn angry. How many fucking lies was he telling me? The first was my name, but why? Why hide that? Then there was a studio no one had ever used which didn't make sense as I was supposed to be a renowned artist. And now the evidence of an affair.

Something was seriously wrong. I needed to know what was in that building. It was definitely important if Dante had the need to lock the door. My stomach churned when I thought of what could actually be in there. I knew he preferred the more kinky sex; maybe it was some sort of dungeon, a BDSM boudoir too extreme to have in the house. Holy hell!

I needed the key. And as Dante opened the door and smiled at me I made a promise that before the night was over, it would no longer be in his pocket, but mine.

CHAPTER 26

RISKS

Dante

SHE WASN'T SUBTLE WITH HER intentions as she sat across from me, her skirt skimming higher up her thigh. She further proved me right when she uncrossed her legs to flash me a pantyless pussy. If I didn't respect her as a doctor and for her discretion in our underworld dealings, I would have pitied her for being so desperate. She knew I was taken. Other men might jump at the chance to fuck her on the side, she was a fetish slut to the max, which I wouldn't lie, appealed to me in the past but that was before Star. Before I felt the ecstasy I achieved in the warmth of her body. No one else had ever given me what she did. The thrill of release, the height of an orgasm so intense I was sure I would never recover after each one.

"Are we done?" I asked Delia when she purposely moved her arm behind her back, pretending to scratch so her breast thrust forward, the peak of a hard nipple pushing through the thin satin material of her shirt.

She blinked at me in confusion as I stood, bored with her relentless flirting. "Oh um, sure."

I gave her a smile as I snatched my shirt from the back of the chair, wincing when the material slid over the small stitch on the underside of my arm. I didn't give her another opportunity to hold me back as I walked through the door, giving her no choice but to follow me.

"I'm taking Star out to dinner," I divulged, another warning for her to back off.

"Is that wise? She may run." She pursed her lips then shrugged. "Although I think even Star would have a problem running on water."

"I'm sure she'll be safe with me." Delia stared at me with a humorous expression. I couldn't hold back the laughter at her look. "Well, maybe not."

She nodded, running her hand up and down my arm, feigning sympathy. "Well, have fun. I hope it's a good night for you both."

I nodded my thanks before I made my way back to the house.

I pulled my phone from my pocket and dialed Malik. "Did you find anything?" I asked as soon as he answered.

"Well, there's talk but that's all."

"Of?"

"Faye."

My teeth clenched with her name. "What?"

"The tattoo."

Fury bubbled through my guts but I pushed past it. "Right."

He tried to say something else but I ended the call. I was still mad at the cunt. It was about time he learnt to keep his desire for his own women, not mine. A smile crept up my lips when a memory of earlier came to me, Malik's lust when he saw me enter Star, his need and pain as he watched me take her in front of him.

Star wasn't waiting for me in the hall and I knew exactly where she would be. The studio. She had surprised me when I found her there earlier. She hadn't managed to create anything other than a mural of paint across one wall, but I knew it would come back to her. I was tempted to find her school art books and show her how fucking good she was. But that would divulge another secret, her name, and I wasn't ready for her to find out yet.

CHAPTER 27

ENTERTAINMENT

Star

THE BOAT ROCKED, NEARLY PLUMMETING me over the side when I stepped into it. Dante's hand shot out to steady me. His humor was vibrant and I couldn't help but feed on it to keep up this mask I held in place to keep him from suspecting that I was feeling anything but in love and happy to be going out with him. I managed a small giggle. I was actually pulling this off despite the raging unrest happening inside. "Thank you." I settled onto one of the tiny seats.

My eyes widened when our driver or pilot or whatever the hell he was called, started pulling away from the island. "Shouldn't we wear those vest things?"

Dante sucked in his lips, trying to stop his laughter at my nerves. "Don't worry, baby. I'll jump in after you." His eyes roamed down my dress, generating a shiver that was nothing to do with the breeze our speed whipped up around me. "And I'm sure you'd look stunning with that dress wet and plastered to your amazing body."

My cheeks flushed. I turned my head to look at the lights twinkling on the mainland. Excitement bubbled in my belly. I was finally out of the house, the warm summer air fresh and filling my lungs.

I ignored the pain in my chest when the vision of my real name followed by Dante and Delia filled my head, her smirk cruel as she pulled her panties up her legs.

"Who is Delia?"

Dante frowned at me, his body tensing. "A friend of ours. Why?"

I shrugged. "I just wondered if she'd managed to find anything else out about my memory loss."

He shook his head and turned away, dismissing me. I sighed and looked back to land, smiling when I realized it grew closer and closer.

I gasped when a gust of wind flicked up the loose material of my dress, my hands pressing against it in my lap to keep it in place.

"Move your hands," Dante ordered.

I gawped at him before flicking my eyes to the driver and shaking my head. He leaned forward and snatched my wrists in his hold. "If I want to look at your pussy, then I will. I don't care where we are, and who is in our company. I own it, Star. I will look at it when and where I please."

My chest heaved. I was sick of his control. I snatched my hands back and glared at him. "I think you'll find I actually own it, not you."

I shivered as darkness descended over him. I pressed against the seat, my fingers gripping the edge hard as the boat swayed when one of his hands seized my neck, his fingers tightening around my throat as his other hand slid straight up my dress, and he tore my panties away with one simple pull.

"Dante!" I choked out.

He ignored me, leaning further into me. "Open your legs." I shook my head, denying him. "Open – your – fucking – legs!"

The driver looked at us over his shoulder. I knew my quarrelling with Dante notified him of our argument more than my surrender would, so I gave in and slowly opened my legs.

Dante immediately dropped his hand from my throat but kept his mouth at my ear. "Your defiance will be the death of both of us. Stop fucking fighting me every step of the way." I nodded, moving my eyes from his. He gripped my chin and tilted my head until I was looking at him. "Don't spoil tonight, Belle."

"I'm sorry," I whispered. I wasn't but I knew my apology was expected. Dante frightened me and if I was to find out what was going on, my constant rebellion would be more of a hindrance.

He regarded me for a moment then nodded and pulled my face towards his, his mouth crashing on mine. I gasped under him, the passion in the kiss a contradiction to the anger that had resided in him not moments ago. Dante's mood was so unpredictable. My surprised gasp turned into a low moan when one of his fingers suddenly thrust inside me, swirling around, stretching my inner walls wide and driving my lust into a dangerous level. I was disappointed in myself for a split second, wishing that we hadn't got company and were whizzing across water in a boat that rocked too much for my liking.

Another finger joined the first, his hand pumping until I instinctively started to grind down on him for more stimulation. I couldn't hold in the loud moan when his thumb pressed against my clit. Cringing at the sound of myself, knowing our chauffeur would have heard me, I kissed Dante harder, trying to disguise my annoying noises.

He reared back to watch me as I became unglued under his touch, his deep eyes observing what he was doing to me. His finger fucking continued, one of his fingers now curled into my front wall, igniting shots of bliss to vibrate in my blood every time he stroked over the sensitive area inside me. He allowed me to lean into him, my mouth biting down on his shoulder to hide my vocal orgasm when he flicked his thumb over my swollen clit, dragging my climax into the stars. I gripped the seat so hard I was frightened of snapping the plastic when every single nerve ending in my body exploded with ecstasy.

"That's it baby, sing for me," he whispered in my ear when I released a long groan of pleasure. I couldn't help it, it was the only way my body could deal with the overload of gratification Dante always gave me with his touch.

The boat slowed then come to a stop as we pulled into a small jetty. Dante slid his fingers from me then brought them to his mouth and slowly ran his tongue up the two fingers that had been inside me before he slipped them fully between his lips and sucked them. His eyes closed and he sighed almost contentedly. "I'm sure nothing will taste as good as you tonight." He smiled when he climbed from the boat and held out his hand to help me step clear.

I nodded, a shiver racing through me. I could feel the flush on my cheeks. The dazed look I knew I wore was the reason for the small smile that erupted into a humorous grin on his face. He winked at me as he gripped my hand and led me up the dock. "Now it's time to feed you."

I sighed. I had fooled him. We were inland. The boyish grin on his face was such a contradiction to the other side of him, the unpredictable side; yet like this, the playful, happy Dante, made my heart swell in my chest. This is who I could believe I had fallen in love with. However, I blinked and frowned to myself when I realized he'd never told me he loved me. Did he?

The discovery caused me to stumble slightly. Dante grabbed me harder, halting my fall. "Jelly legs?" He laughed.

"Yeah." I nodded with a forced smile. "Something like that."

I couldn't keep my hungry eyes in my head as we meandered up a few streets, the cobbled road under my heels generating a few more stumbles. Dante held me up, his arm secure around my waist.

"Where are we?" I asked as I peered into numerous shop windows. He didn't answer me and I turned to him. He smiled but still didn't answer. "Dante, where are we?" I repeated, to be greeted with more silence.

I shook off the anger at his ignorance and continued to keep my attention on the variety of goods adorning the mass of stores along our journey. Large stones, a pretty blue in color with specks of red were displayed in every single window and I assumed it to be specific to the island. Pebble jewelry and ornaments incorporated it. I needed to get online, which Dante had so far refused, to find this stone's origin.

Dante led me across the road and into a small door. The lighting was subdued, almost too low as we walked through another door. We were welcomed immediately by a tall man in a black suit. "Mr. Troy," he greeted with what sounded like a French accent, thrusting his hand

139

towards Dante.

I frowned as my gaze roamed the entirety of the room. It was completely empty apart from a couple sat at the back and two men engrossed in conversation at a center table.

"Bernard." Dante smiled widely, taking the man's hand in his. "Thank you for doing this."

"It is my pleasure, sir." He turned to me with a large toothy smile. "Miss." He swept a hand out to the side, towards the middle of the room. "If you'd care to follow me, your table is ready."

Dante pressed a hand to my lower back and directed me after Bernard who led us towards a small round table to the back of the room. It didn't escape my notice we were also seated away from the front of the restaurant and windows.

A man stood from his table when we passed. Dante stiffened so much I thought his spine was going to snap in two.

"Well, well. Good evening, Troy." He turned his sneer to me and I shivered. "And your lovely fiancé. Star, isn't it?" He was mocking me for some reason.

"Yes, sir," I answered politely. He knew me as Star…

His gaze roamed my body, a sickening smirk on his face. "Out for dinner?"

What the hell was this guy's problem? What did he think we were doing there?

Dante slid his fingers around my arm. I winced when they tightened to bruising point. "Yes, Davies. Now if you'll excuse us, we would like our privacy. If we had wanted company, I would have made sure not to alert you to it anyway."

It was my turn to stiffen this time with Dante's harsh tone and harsher words.

Fury covered Davies' face but Dante didn't wait for him to reply before he continued to lead me over to our own table. I gawped at him but he appeared completely relaxed, smiling at me as he pulled out my chair for me to sit.

After we were seated, Bernard lifted the bottle of champagne out of the bucket on the table and proceeded to fill our glasses before he placed it back in the ice then left us to it. I scanned our surroundings again to check for more people, an exit maybe I could slip out of. I could find somewhere safe and then call Dante to tell him I needed time.

Dante smiled at me over the rim of his glass, and as if sensing my question, he answered before it was asked. "I paid for us to have privacy but Davies. He's a hanger-on. With you being in the public eye, and because he knows me, he thinks it entitles him to some of the notoriety. He's a fame hungry vulture."

Nodding and forcing a smile, I tipped the glass and took a sip of bubbly. It hit my stomach and forced its way back up instantly. I spluttered, coughing like a fool and spitting the yellow liquid all over the table.

Dante shot up, his hand gently slapping my back. "Are you okay?"

I nodded, laughing lightly to hide my embarrassment. "I think it went down the wrong hole."

He continued to rub my back for a while before he sat back down and stared at me across the table. The conversation was stilted and I gazed around the room, giving my thoughts something other than Dante and Delia to focus on, but they struggled to remain inside me, like the champagne. I snapped my eyes to his and bit the bullet. "Why were you putting your shirt back on when you came out of that building with Delia?"

His eyes widened before they darkened and a small tic twitched furiously in his cheek. He leaned forwards on the table, his fist propping up his chin as he glared at me. "Have you been spying on me, Belle?"

"What? No, the studio window looks directly over that way, I couldn't really miss it… or the way Delia made sure I saw her slip her panties back up her fucking legs!"

He blinked at me in confusion. "What?"

"Oh, don't deny it, Dante. I saw you both. The smug bitch made sure she had my attention, a dirty fucking smile on her ugly fucking face as she shimmied them over her legs."

I lifted my chin proudly. Wow, I was feisty. I liked it.

His confused expression morphed into one of humor. He tipped his head, studying me intently. "I do believe you're jealous."

My mouth popped open. "Of course I'm jealous. You're my fiancé… or so you keep telling me. Forgive me if I'm wrong but I actually thought when you're marrying someone that makes you kind of exclusive. I'm not into open relationships, Dante. Nor will I ever be!"

I couldn't work out if he wanted to laugh or smack the living hell out of me. He was silent for a while, his eyes dark and intense, making me squirm as I waited for his reaction. I knew this relationship was far from normal, but shit, any other woman who watched the man they were about to marry walk out of a building putting his shirt back on while a bitch pulled on her panties had a right to be fucking mad.

My body stiffened instinctively when Dante slowly stood up and walked around the table. I kept my body braced for his fury, my eyes fixed on the table as my teeth furiously savaged my bottom lip. I gasped when he dropped to his haunches beside my chair.

"Star." I swallowed hard before I shifted my gaze to him. His face was soft, causing me to frown. Was it part of his game; give me a false sense of security before he beat the feisty out of me? "Baby, I have never, nor will I ever in this lifetime or the next slip my dick into the doc." He took my hand, running his thumb softly over my knuckles. "Yes, she has a thing for me… I mean who wouldn't?" he joked. "And the only reason I was slipping my shirt back on was because Delia is using me as a guinea pig for one of her drug trials." My brow creased when he stood up, slipped his jacket off then started to unbutton his shirt. He turned marginally and lifted his arm. A small suturing stitch sat just below his armpit. As though checking it was real, I reached up and ran my finger gently over it.

"Oh."

He lifted a brow. "Are we okay now?" He re-dressed then slid back into his seat, continuing to watch me as he took another drink.

"Why was she slipping her panties back on?"

A waitress appeared beside us and I blinked up at her as though she'd appeared out of thin air. Heat flooded my cheeks, hoping she hadn't overheard my question. She turned to smile at me. One of the plates slid from her hands and crashed onto the floor, her mouth as wide as the area the food covered on the plush carpet. "Oh my God," she choked out. "It's…"

"What the fuck?" Dante exploded as he shot upright. "You stupid bitch!"

Bernard hurried over, his round head shaking from side to side. "Gabrielle!" he barked. "Clean this mess up at once!" He turned to Dante, his palms crushed together as though he was praying… maybe he was. "I'm so, so sorry, Mr. Troy. Gabrielle is feeling a little under the weather today."

"Miss Avery," Gabrielle whispered.

"Miss Avery!"

Someone shouted from the masses as I stepped out of the limo. Cameras went off everywhere, their flashes blinding and somewhat annoying. "Faye!" various people screamed as I placed my feet on the long red carpet.

"I love you!"

"Please, marry me."

"You're so beautiful!"

"Faye!"

"Faye, can I have your autograph?"

I blinked furiously at the screams, the lights, the noise, the atmosphere, all of it overwhelming but usual.

"Keep moving, Faye," Frank urged as he slipped an arm around my waist and directed me into the building, Tony flanking the other side as Dave led our group.

"Good evening, Miss Avery," the head of house greeted, her large, white toothy smile almost as blinding as the camera lights. "If you'd care to follow me, I'll show you to your seat."

We continued behind her as she looked over her shoulder to me. "I must say, I'm rather excited about this showing."

I smiled at her. "Thank you."

"We've seated you next to Mr. Troy." She gave me a wink and I clenched my teeth.

Frank's arm tightened. "Keep it in, Faye. They don't know nothing, it's just gossip." I nodded without looking at him. I liked Frank, he was a father figure, a friend, and I trusted him implicitly.

A woman rushed out from nowhere and before I could blink I was covered head to toe in a mass of what looked and smelled like egg and milk.

"You whore!" she spat. "You will burn in hell!"

My eyes, although sticky, widened on her when Frank and Tony wrestled her to the ground. Security guards from everywhere stormed the foyer.

"A woman's body is holy, she must never reveal its secrets," she continued to rant as they pulled her away. "You spill your secrets to the world. You are going to hell!"

I smiled at her and rolled my eyes. "For fuck's sake," I murmured with a weary sigh to Frank. "Anyone would think I'd filmed a porno."

He chuckled, his head shaking from left to right. "You never know, Faye. Things might be looking up."

I elbowed him in the ribs, his laughter growing as Theo rushed over to us. Frank's laugh stopped immediately as his body tensed. "Oh watch out, here comes, Jack."

I shushed him, trying to hide the giggle at his Jack the Ripper nickname he had christened Theo with.

"What the hell happened here?" Theo barked at our escort.

"Someone needs to help Miss Avery out of her ruined dress," a voice said from behind me. I tried to hide the smile from my face before I turned to see my fiancé looking at me with a quirked brow. I knew he found all this amusing and I glared at him.

"Thank you, Mr. Troy. I'll get right to it. Please excuse me."

"Are you sure you can manage on your own?" he asked, his eyes lit with laughter as they roamed over my now yellow and white red dress. "There are a few guys out there who would love to help." He gestured with his thumb to the crowd outside.

"You smell adorable," he whispered in my ear when he leaned into me. I shook my head and sighed.

"Be grateful I'm not jumping you here in the foyer."

His tongue pushed into his cheek as he nodded. "I'm game, baby."

"Ssh." I giggled as I followed our escort's lead into one of the side rooms. Her eyes and ears didn't miss a thing.

"You and Mr. Troy make an adorable couple," she gushed as she helped me out of my dress.

"We're just friends," I said quickly.

"Of course you are." She winked back at me.

"For fuck's sake!" Dante's loud voice broke me from the memory. "Get this cleaned up and bring us some more food."

Bernard nodded eagerly. "Yes, thank you, sir. The meal, of course, is now on the house."

"I should think so. And don't expect a recommendation!" Dante fumed. I blinked, looking around for our waitress but she had disappeared.

"I'm so sorry, baby." Dante growled. "I wanted tonight to be special."

My gut twisted at the tone in his voice, it was angry but also sad. "It will be." I smiled at him, I was learning who I was. "It was only the starter. By the time we get to dessert, Bernard will need a new carpet." I winked at him, trying to lighten the situation.

His lips twisted before he started to chuckle. "Then I think we need to get to the main course."

I frowned at him. "I need a starter first."

He ignored me and stood up, pulling his jacket back into place. I stared wide-eyed, my jaw dropping when he took a big breath and dropped to one knee by my side. He took my hand and slowly looked up at me.

"I know we're already engaged but I need to do this, to once again signify our relationship. We've been together since the beginning of my memories, Star. I can't lose you, I refuse to lose you. I know the past few weeks have been... challenging and I promised, as I still promise, to get us through to our future. Because that's all I see, a future with both of us in."

My heart thundered in my chest. My throat was restricted, making it difficult for my lungs to do their job. My mind was a chaotic mess, making everything hazy and dreamlike. He reached into his inner pocket and retrieved a small blue velvet box. When he flicked the lid open, I peered at the gold band, a huge blue sapphire glued to the top. It was hideous. It wasn't me or my taste. I recognized my memories failed me but I knew I would never have gone for anything so gaudy.

"What...?" I took a deep breath. "Where's the other ring?"

He blinked at me, his teeth grinding so hard I could hear the scrape of them over each other. But he ignored my question. "Marry me, Star. Give yourself to me, all of you. Show me you love me."

His selfish proposal stuck in my throat. What happened to his previous adoring one, the one my memories actually allowed me to remember? His loving words, his worship as he slid the ring onto my finger down a piece of string?

"I want you to propose like you did last time. When the time is right. When I know who I am." I hadn't wanted to say it but my brain hadn't told my mouth.

"Like last time?" He echoed my words, his eyes turning black as his face paled. His eyes were curious, almost accusing as his head tipped to the side and he scrutinized me like I had stabbed him in the back.

I nodded faintly, aware I had pushed too far.

"I remembering little by little. I remembered a number earlier when you answered it's all coming back Dante I just need more time." To stall! I didn't voice the last part. He stood up slowly, his action causing my body to brace itself. He brushed at his suit, his fingers sweeping the material as though removing lint that wasn't there.

"You know," he said quietly, too quietly. "The previous proposal is forgotten, Star. I don't care how I proposed last time; I was trying to make a fresh start here." His voice was growing louder, his tone deeper, his fury higher. "But as usual, you have to spoil it, just like you ruin every other – fucking – thing – I – try – to – do." I squealed loudly when he snatched a large handful of my hair and hauled me out of the chair. "I'm sick and tired of your selfishness." My hands lifted to his as I tried to prise my hair from his fingers, the pull burning my scalp. My knees thudded on the floor as he dragged me across the room.

Bernard stared at us with shock, his huge round eyes and the other diners' following our journey out of his restaurant. Davies smirked as though amused at my refusal.

"Dante," I hissed when my knees scraped over the cobbles. I attempted to stand, but his powerful hold pushed me back to the floor. "I will," I cried. "I'll marry you. I'm sorry." My hands clawed at the stones beneath me until I resembled a dog on all fours scurrying along beside him.

He scoffed and shook his head. "I'm not sure I want you anymore. You're nothing but a selfish whore! And in front of fucking Davies of all cunts to be there. He will find this so funny!"

"I'm sorry!" I choked out as tears blinded my way, not that I needed to see where I was going with Dante's stern navigation. A man outside a bar, smoking, gawped at us as we passed.

"Hey!" he shouted. "Are you okay?"

Dante stilled immediately then turned, his body tensing further. "Keep out of this."

The guy stepped forward. "You're hurting her. She's not a dog!" His voice was low, accusing but confident. "Let her go and we'll forget all about this."

Dante scoffed, a cold chill emanating from him. "I don't think we will forget all about this." Malik suddenly appeared behind us. Where the hell had he come from?

I gasped as the guy held up his hands when Malik pulled out a gun and trained it on the guy's head. "Whoa!"

"Malik!" I wheezed. "What are you doing?"

His eyes shot to mine and his brow creased as he struggled with his own actions. He shifted his gaze to Dante, then back to the random. "Go back inside if you want to continue living."

This wasn't Malik. He was suddenly cruel and as twisted as Dante. "Malik. Put the gun away!"

I was flung upright, my body heaving with Dante's manipulation. "Shut the fuck up! You've caused enough trouble tonight!"

I never found out what happened next. Dante's fist crashed into my head and everything went black.

CHAPTER 28

MEMORY LANE

Star

"IT HURTS SO MUCH," I sobbed.

"What can I do, Faye? I feel so helpless." He crawled up onto the bed I was lying on. His warm protective body curved around mine. "You didn't have to go through with this, Faye. He would have done the right thing."

I moved my arm to grip on to his. "I couldn't do this to him. He has a future, this would have ruined it. What if he didn't do the right thing? You know how he can get."

I felt his disapproval varnishing me. "Then I would have." It was a whisper falling forbiddingly from his lips. My eyes closed, refusing to let my mind wander into that impossibility. I turned to face him. He was so beautiful ...Dante?

"Yes it's me. I'm sorry Star." My eyes fluttered open; he was older than he was in my dream. A throb on the side of my head began a steady thump. My knees screamed for some relief. "I've got the doctor coming to dress your knees. I lost it. I'm sorry. You pushed me... you just keep pushing." Exhaling the breath I'd been holding, I didn't look directly at him

"I don't want that woman touching me. I can see to my own needs." My stomach stirred and I knew I couldn't swallow down the rising vomit.

I sprinted from the bed. Ignoring the disapproval from my knees, I dropped down over the toilet just in time for my stomach to eject everything inside it, which wasn't much. The retch tightened my stomach muscles so forcibly it reminded me of the pain I felt in the dream.

The younger image of Dante once again clouded my mind, his gentle touch and tone. The younger man was a complete contradiction to the older version.

I felt him before he actually made himself known. "The doctor will be here in ten minutes. You're sick."

Pulling myself to my feet I shook my head. "I said I don't want her here."

He stepped towards me. I cowered, making him stop. "You don't have to be afraid of me, Star."

Was he serious? I could barely stand. I needed courage. I couldn't let him turn me into this.

"I won't be a victim for you to lose control on, Dante. This," I pointed to the bruise I knew marred my face, then down to my scraped bloodied knees. "I don't know what I did wrong." I sounded weak to my own ears, my voice barely a whisper. The truth was, he flipped a switch and was once again the man from when I first woke up with no memories in that holding cell. It was terrifying. Where was the man I had memories of? Where was the man in my dreams? *Where were you? Why did you abandon me?* My enigma, haunting me. I was drowning in the unknown.

"You keep searching for a past that doesn't matter now! You may not remember it but I do and I don't want us to be who we were then. Things are different now and this is your life NOW, so you fighting me, trying to recreate a past is meaningless to the NOW! It's getting old!" Every word travelled across the air to attack me like a physical slap.

"Now you're sick, let the doctor look at you," he continued once his temper had simmered back down again.

"It will just be something I ate," I mocked. I hadn't had a chance to actually eat anything before I was dragged from the restaurant.

His eyes lowered to slits. I was being bold and brave considering what he had done to me earlier. There was a woman inside me who was defiant and she wanted to smash through the walls. Her voice was faint, but grew louder and louder every day.

I knew he was angry; it was derived from a fury, not just from that one sentence. He was mad at me or at everything. Fuck only knew what made him this way but something had because the man who lived in my memories was not the one simmering on the edge of rage in front of me.

"She's here." Malik's voice came from behind Dante and then a hand came up to his chest, red nail polish blazing from each perfected nail.

"Let me by," she cooed. She was too personal with him and the cheek of her over-familiar hands was an insult to me. How dare she come into my house, claim we were friends and then act like she had a secret with MY fiancé? How dare he raise his hand to me and treat me the way he did?

He moved aside and she made sure to get as close as possible as she shimmied against his body. Even her cheeks were tinted red with lust, the freaking whore. Screw that.

She smirked and turned to me, eyeing me up and down and tutting. Her whorish mouth opened. "Oh dear, Star. Let's get you cleaned up. What happened?" Like she didn't know.

It happened like I wasn't in my own body, a reflex. My hand balled into a fist, reared back and flew at her full force. The crunch I felt under my hand was fucking amazing.

Blood exploded like a paint gun bullet hitting a target. Her head sprang backwards and her body followed, leaving her screaming on her back.

"That happened, only it was a little harder and to the right. Don't worry about cleaning me up. You should clean yourself up."

Stepping around her, I pinned Dante with a glare. "If you want that ring on my finger, you'll keep this whore out of my house and out of your bed!" I spat, moving past him. My heart stammered inside my rib-cage when he grabbed my wrist, halting my retreat. I didn't turn to look at him, I just held my breath.

"I told you she hasn't been in my bed. It was the truth. I'll get her out of here and you won't have to see her again." I released the breath and nodded my head. "You will put the ring on and we'll forget tonight happened."

He released my wrist, and I moved my feet forward, shooting Malik a glare. He had proved I was alone in this. He worked and was friends with Dante, not me. I was just his friend's property.

I went to the studio, locking the door behind me. My legs gave out and I crumbled to the floor, wrapping my arms around my knees.

I allowed the tears to come. They came with a wave of loneliness. I felt incomplete, like I was back in that cell. My heart felt empty, missing someone who was not there anymore.

CHAPTER 29

WHO AM I?

Star

"I HAVE A SURPRISE FOR you."

I giggled as I stared at the almost-naked man in front of me; the only thing covering his privates was a magazine with me on the front cover. "If I have already seen it, it's not a surprise and, Mr. Troy, that," I pointed to where he was covered, "is something I have definitely seen... felt... and tasted." I winked, loving the lust in his gaze.

My teeth sank into my lip when he took a step towards me. "They advised no visible name tattoos right?" he murmured, making my blood heat every part of my body.

"No!" I screeched.

"Ssh, it's okay. It's me. I'm moving you to our bed." My body protested. Aches from the earlier trauma, and from falling asleep on the floor of the studio burst into my sleepy state, making me groan.

"Ssh." The sound was comforting, familiar. My body came down against the soft mattress. Swiping my hair from my face, he handed me a glass of water. "Open your mouth, Belle. I have some pain relief for you."

I swallowed the pills with a gulp of water and succumbed to the beckoning dreams. Where I was happy, and Dante was too.

I awoke early, the sunrise breathing its light through the room. Dante was asleep next to me, which was surprising. Slowly climbing from the bed, I relieved my bladder before showering yesterday away from me.

As I stepped out, Dante stepped in. He stopped me from leaving with a gentle voice, almost like a plea. "Stay in with me."

I wasn't used to the soft side of him; it confused me, played with my head. His eyes fixed on mine, something similar to pain burning its way through them.

I let him wash me for a second time, his touch leaving the usual burn in my core. I refused to give in to it. He hurt me, humiliated me. I felt like I was floating in space, looking down at the world I used to be a part of.

The cold, dark abyss swallowed me, pulling me further and further from the earth, from breaking the atmosphere and being who I once was. A deep ache inside me told me this wasn't where I was supposed to be and I was more lost than ever before.

Stepping free, ignoring the sigh from Dante, I dried off and slipped into some jeans and a tee.

Dante told me he would be gone for most of the day when he came from the bathroom with only a towel wrapped around his waist. Images assaulted me of another time.

"You can't keep fighting it, Faye."

He walked towards me, the tiny towel barely covering him. The water pellets beaded over every inch of his skin, crying at me to lick them. I wanted to taste each drop, savor and devour him under my tongue.

"Fighting what?" I didn't trust myself to say anything more without panting.

"Us!" He groaned in frustration, dropping the towel and making my breath hitch. "I've waited long enough, Faye. I can't bear it any longer. I need you. You can't deny what's between us anymore. I crave to hear your voice. I sense you before you even enter a room because I'm not complete when you're not with me. You set every nerve on fire whenever you touch me. I want to grab onto you and burn up in everything we could be. I want to explore every inch of you; I want to feel you come undone under my tongue. I want to feel you around my cock as I make love to you. I want you. Just let yourself love me back." He stepped closer, igniting a stream of goosebumps to explode over my sensitive skin. "I'm so unbelievably in love with you. I can't fucking breathe until I see you some days. I feel you in me so deep we're two halves of the same soul."

A tear slipped down my cheek. A knocking at the door broke the spell.

"Mr. Troy, you're needed in thirty minutes."

"Star, what the fuck! Where did you go?" I blinked up at Dante.

"Two halves of the same soul."

He raised an eyebrow. "What?"

I shook my head.

For an hour I looked through every box and drawer in our room and there was nothing, not even an old yearbook. Diary. Photos. Documents. Birth certificate. Nothing. I knew I needed to search his office but Malik was there. I had to get him out of the house. I tried the phone line but there was no dial tone this time.

Making my way down the stairs, I followed the scent of bacon. The sizzling lifted more aromas into the air and the smell made my stomach churn. I couldn't hold it in. Turning to the sink I retched, my eyes watering, my body vibrating with the clammy fever that comes with sickness.

A heavy palm came down to rub my shoulder. "Star, you still sick?"

My head filled with fog. I wasn't sick! Why would that scent have made me … No…? NO! Thinking back over the time since I had woken up, I hadn't had a period. But Dante was so flippant with not using protection, I assumed I was covered with the jab or implant …no. Oh God, no.

I turned to the worried expression of Malik. Wiping my mouth with the back of my hand, I tried to offer him a small smile. "If I asked you to do something for me would you? No questions asked and without telling Dante?"

He shifted his eyes to the floor.

"Please," I croaked, gripping onto his arm.

"What is it?"

I looked around for the camera I knew was in there and turned my back to it, whispering. "A pregnancy test."

His intake of breath was audible. He nodded and sighed.

"Thank you."

I watched him leave on the outdoor monitor an hour later, after calling the boy who came to get everyone, and as soon as the boat faded from view, I began my search of Dante's office. But he was a clever bastard, or a paranoid one, because there was nothing in there, not even a solitary household bill.

I picked up his pen holder in frustration and threw it across the room, watching as it fell by the window. Counting to ten I calmed myself and walked across the room to pick it up. The moss covered building I saw him leave that day came into view, making my heart jump.

I snatched up his letter opener and rushed through the house, across the distance separating us and tried the lock. It was locked. Trying to pick a lock was harder than it looked on TV.

I tried again, digging the sharp end into the keyhole and twitching it… nothing. Screw it! I looked around for a stone or rock and found a plant pot. There was no way I could make an excuse for this to him but I would take the repercussions. Something inside told me I needed to get into that damn building if I was to ever find out who I was… who Dante was.

I lifted the stone, took a deep breath, and with as much strength as I could muster I launched it through the window. The shattering sound splintered the silence. My nerves vibrated through my entire body.

I pushed the rest of the glass out of the way and climbed through the panel, cutting my palm as I hooked my fingers around the frame to give me some leverage inside.

It looked like an office. A desk and office equipment was tucked away neatly against each wall; numerous pictures hung from the walls and a plush carpet covered the floor. Adjoining doors led to another room but none of this filtered inside my head. None of these things registered as my gaze fell to a table and my body slammed to a halt.

A suitcase was flipped open, a few items of clothing still folded neatly inside. Toiletries and even a camera sat idly inside. I recognized it. Like a snapshot of pictures, some memories filtered in. The suitcase belonged to me… I was traveling on a plane.

Taking small steps over to it, I brushed my fingers over the leather and picked up the label.

Faye Avery.

Tears dropped to my cheek. My scent. Cherry blossom… my old scent filled my senses. I picked up the notes laid on top.

My body
needs you.

Make sure you send me a
selfie... of that smile when
you touch yourself to
thoughts of me.

Put this on your dressing room mirror! You are beautiful and I love every perfect inch of you, even that inch you hate ;) Love you more than life. I'm going to marry the shit out of you, Faye Avery... soon to be Troy.

It didn't make sense. Nothing did. I wasn't supposed to be there.

My chest throbbed reading those messages. The hole expanding in my chest grew ever wider, the cold seeping free. I couldn't reach the most important memory, the one that would answer this lonely feeling inside me.

Panicking I was going to run out of time, I quickly slipped the notes into my jeans and rushed back to the house to wait out Malik's return.

CHAPTER 30

DÉJÀ VU

Star

I GRIPPED MY HAIR, TUGGING frantically at my soft curls as memory after memory assaulted me. For the previous hour, they had been slamming into me; old ones, new ones, devastating ones, confusing ones, happy ones, all of them one after the other, minute after minute. I felt dizzy with them all, nauseous, as each one destroyed me a little more inside.

I had prayed for the return of my memories, but now, now I wasn't sure I wanted them back. They were annihilating me, burning my mind under the chaos of them all and breaking my heart little by little after each one.

Dante loved me. He was caring and so utterly gentle that each vision of him clashed with what my heart now knew of him.

I couldn't understand, or find the memory that had changed him into the bitter and twisted man he was now. All that came to me were recollections of our teenage years and very early twenties; school days, day trips, happy moments, erotic time spent buried in each other. None of them, not one, was of him angry, or forceful in bed. He was besotted with me, completely worshipped me.

What the hell had happened between then and now? I needed this memory more than any of the other ones. Although they were enlightening, none of them told me anything new, all of them virtually the same as the previous, each one showing me the love Dante and I had shared.

"Hey." Malik's gentle voice filtered through my muddled brain.

I blinked up at him, forcing away another painful memory. "Did you get it?"

He nodded and held a small white paper bag in front of him and away from the camera in the corner of the ceiling. We exchanged a look for a moment. Both of us pained by what we knew was to come.

I pushed off the couch and walked over to him, coming to stand directly in front of him, his body blocking the camera. Taking the bag from him, I snatched a pen from the bureau.

What the hell is going on?

He stared at my writing scrawled over the paper bag. He blinked at it, his brow creased. Lifting his eyes to mine, he swallowed. "Nothing."

I narrowed my eyes at his lie.

"Fair enough."

His eyes closed, denying me access to the guilt in his gaze. "Star..."

"Faye!" I whispered, correcting him.

His jaw dropped. I didn't give him chance to answer as I pushed past him and fled up the stairs, anger surging through me with his reticence, however it came as no great shock. Dante owned Malik just as much as he owned me. We weren't his family or his friends. We were possessions, things to control and manipulate for his own sick, perverted desires.

The bathroom walls seemed to close in on me when I shut and locked the door behind me. Staring at the bag, I wasn't sure I wanted to do the test. I already knew what it would say. Tears sprung from my eyes before I had even peed on the damn thing.

I couldn't have a baby with Dante, not the Dante he was now. The old one, hell yes, very much so, but not now. This baby had been created from nothing more than a vicious and cruel fetish of his, one he had blamed me for. He had said it was my fantasy, but I knew there was no way this was me. I had no proof, only my own gut feeling deep down this wasn't an experiment gone wrong.

Dante had told me he was being used as a guinea pig for the lovely Doc, and I wondered if that was what this was, an experiment gone wrong, me as the guinea pig this time. I was nothing more than a lab rat.

Pulling the box from the bag, I ran my thumb over the writing as another memory flooded in.

"I can't do this."

"You have to," he said sternly beside me. "You need to know, as he does... as I do."

I frowned at him. How would the result affect him? I shook off his words and turned, disappearing into the bathroom, the long pink box weighing heavy in my hands.

He stood waiting for me when I came back out, wringing his hands together nervously. He took one look at my ashen face, the tears that fell, and opened his arms to me.

"Ssh," he whispered when I fell into him and sobbed. "It will be okay, Faye. I promise."

I gasped, pulling much needed air into my lungs as a shudder shot through me. That had been the most confusing memory of them all. My thoughts at wondering how the results would affect him.

I shook my head, pushing them away, knowing I would go crazy if I dwelled on them. Taking another deep breath, I pulled the test from the box and nodded to myself sternly.

161

I was surprised to see Malik staring at me when I slowly opened the bathroom door and walked back into the bedroom, my legs trembling as my heart beat too fast.

"Well?"

I shook my head rapidly, sweat from the despair flowing through me flicking off my forehead. I knew what it would say, but the proof was too much. A long high pitched wail left me as my life changed so very swiftly with the appearance of one pale blue cross.

"Star," Malik whispered, his expression one of utter desolation. "Star." He took a step towards me but I stepped back and hissed.

"Tell me what's going on!"

His face crumbled. "I can't." His pained whisper was enough to tell me I was on my own. "Please, Star," he urged desperately when a sob echoed from me.

I couldn't breathe, the room closed in on me as my ears started whooshing. Malik took another step towards me. I flew for him, anger at everything coming to a head as I smashed fist after fist into him. He stood and tolerated it, allowed me vent it all on him. His body was my punching bag as I pummeled him, my tears and snot as furious as my hits.

I knew Malik cared for me, but his loyalty and love for Dante was much greater.

"No!" I screamed when his arms came around me. I pushed him off and slapped his face, the final piece of anger forcing itself out.

His palm lifted to his face as the sting shot through him.

"Faye! My name is Faye! Fuck you!" I spat out. "FUCK YOU ALL!! I'm done!"

I fled through the house. Whatever the outcome, I was leaving, whether I had to fucking swim to land, whether I drowned in the water's depths, I didn't care anymore. I couldn't bear another second in this house, never mind the rest of my life. Whether my memory came back or not was irrelevant, I wanted to be free of the oppressive bastard who had done this to me.

The walls rushed past me as my legs carried me faster and faster. My heart beat too fast and I lifted my hand, pressing it to my chest to try and alleviate the pain burning my heart.

The door slammed back into its frame when I burst through it. The grass under my bare feet was almost sensual, its softness calming and encouraging me to run faster and faster.

Yet the world shifted when I finally made it to the small dock and I skidded on the damp ground when flashes and shouts blinded me.

CHAPTER 31

ENTRAPMENT

Dante

I WAS SO TENSE. I knew what she had asked Malik to get for her on land. She thought she had an ally in him and in some ways she did. But he knew the hand that fed him was also the one that wouldn't hesitate to break his neck if he crossed me. He respected her and held affection he tried to suppress but didn't ... couldn't. She was infectious; once she was in your blood there was no way you could ever get her out. I was a prime example.

I fell in love with an eleven year old Star. I remembered first seeing her in the cast of the moon's glow. The removal trucks were still moving her family in to the house she lived in from that day forward. Even after the sun had set they continued to move furniture inside.

I lived a few streets over in a nicer area. Her smile lifted to me when she noticed me. I was late home and my dad was going to ground me but I couldn't move. I was only thirteen but I felt it, a jolt, a connection. Her mum dragged her inside.

I had stared at the house until long after the removal truck left, waiting, and then the curtain twitched and green eyes looked back at me.

The next day she showed up at my school. She walked straight up to me in the cafeteria and placed a drawing in front of me. It was of me on my bike outside her house. It was so lifelike; she had even captured the infatuated look in my eyes. How could someone so young draw so well?

All eyes went to this new brazen girl who'd placed her tray next to mine and sat amongst all my friends. "Hey, I'm Faye!" She beamed, reaching her hand out to me. I blinked a few times before taking it in my palm. I looked down and noticed a faint birthmark on her wrist. "It's the shape of a star," I murmured. Her eyebrow rose but I smiled, turned to everyone and told them, "This is, Star. She's with me."

For six years she was by my side, we were a unit. I was different from most of our friends; there was something inside me that set me apart from everyone emotionally, everyone but her. I had issues with authority and it all stemmed from never feeling like I fit in amongst my family. My father was in the entertainment business and wanted the same fate for his children but it never appealed to me.

I had an IQ of 160; I was more intelligent than most of the teachers at our school but my parents didn't send me to private school to master my intellect. They believed public school taught value and a backbone, so despite their wealth, that was where I went.

Science interested me, and luckily I had an amazing teacher who knew what to do with me, and who to contact for colleges. When I was approached for an internship with a major pharmaceutical company and college scholarship, my parents didn't even congratulate me. Any other parents would have thrown a party, cried a little and told their kid they were proud, but I got nothing. Star did all those things. She was willing to put our future on hold while I went to college.

Little did I know it was so she could fuck *him* behind my back without the fear of getting caught. She didn't even wait for me to leave the state before she went to *him*. The day I planned to tell her I gave it all up because I couldn't be away from her.

I'd do what my father wanted and go to community college and then go into entertainment like him. I bought her a ring and held my tongue all through my farewell party the night before. She had said her goodbyes the night before because she couldn't bear seeing me drive away. Fucking lying bitch.

The next evening after I planned everything out for her proposal, I drove towards her house but slowed to a stop when I saw her leaving her house with *him*. I followed them to a motel. I was dizzy; my world tipped on its axel. My insides twisted and threatened to leave my body. How could she do this to me? How could *THEY* do this? She was mine, she had always been mine. I fucking loved her. I breathed for her; she was the only person who believed in me. I took her for who she was. I kept her safe from her horrid mother. I gave her everything she wanted, including my heart.

I couldn't breathe, but when I finally did inhale it wasn't air, it was vengeance. I switched it off, everything I felt for her. I incinerated it inside me and let the embers sizzle with new-found hate in my heart. They were all mocking me and they would all pay for it. Fuck my parents. Fuck her and fuck the cunt fucking her.

I waited outside their motel until the sun set and rose. Then I left and never went back.

I ditched my phone, my only communication to her so she couldn't ever reach inside me and touch what she had broken. What they had all broken.

When the plane I was supposed to be on that day had engine failure and dropped from the sky, exploding into a ball of flames on impact, no one waited to have confirmation I was on the plane, they assumed, accepted and told everyone I was dead. How could people who are engineered to love their children just accept one's death without knowing for sure? How could a girl who shared my soul for six years not wait, not come looking for me?

My love for her saved and destroyed me all in one day.

A month later they were informed I had never boarded the plane and was very much alive. Not even then did one of them come looking for me. That was the final cut to let the ruthless bastard I harbored under the surface take the reins of my life. I embraced the other side of myself. I fed it with the betrayal I felt so deep inside me; the craving for vengeance was always there waiting for an opportunity.

I built myself a name. Worked through an internship and finished college two years earlier than it took most people. I was determined and focused. I was given a full time position when my internship finished and I worked up the ranks quickly, honing my skills, making a name for myself and then I slipped into the darker dealings of my craft and made my empire.

Years went by with no contact and then I almost choked when I first saw her on TV. It was a commercial for God knows what; all I could hear was my own heart beat banging in my ears and all I saw were those green eyes, mocking me. She had done what everyone else wanted her to do. She became an actress instead of the artist she was created to be.

The anger and ache of betrayal surfaced. I watched her grow from a nothing into a starlet. Commercial after commercial, then into films until she was known worldwide alongside …*HIM*. They never admitted to being couple to the media. Their agent's assistant, Theo, told me it was the agents who made them keep their relationship secret. They were worth more single and got more privacy that way.

The hate festered, growing darker and more urgent but I had waited long enough. I needed to wait for the right time and the right method of payback but I didn't plan on it being as brutal as it became until fate stepped in.

Six months previous

"The drug's ready, everything is set up. We just need to decide on the target and money of course." I quirked a brow and thought back to how we ended up here. Ten men congregated around the table in the back of the restaurant Davies had chosen for us to eat at.

We were going to leave business until after dinner when we were in the privacy of my office but the little runt wouldn't stop asking questions. I wasn't a fan of the slave trade but unfortunately, when you played in the underworld, Hades' true nature dwelled there and that was the sex trade.

I usually dealt in the drugs. I made them and distributed them. I dealt in truth serums, drugs that numbed certain areas and not others. Drugs to bring on death without evidence of cause. Those were my side projects. I had finished working on a new drug to remove the bad feelings associated with traumatic events, taking away painful memories. 'Fear extinction'. It could help rid sufferers of post-traumatic stress and phobias from their anxiety and trauma.

Medical boards all wanted their hands on the goods. My name was in medical media everywhere. I loved the power, but it wasn't enough. I tweaked the drug, suppressing all memories and leaving the brain open to suggestion, to re-learn, to be molded and corrupted, and let the world's most immoral bid on its exclusivity.

When Hunter approached me with a proposal for a new business, it was power of a whole new level. We would start a secret club of the world's most rich and powerful, but also people who we knew were depraved and had kinks and urges that needed to be fed in the shadows of society. They would all have access to vote on a target. Someone desired by them or millions, or just a payback from one of our wealthier clients who wanted a personal arrangement.

When you fucked over these men, they harbored revenge until they could exact it in the most destructive way possible. I admired that because I was the same way. What better way than to take one of their enemies' women and change her memories, make her a whore or make her fall in love with you to spite him. The possibilities were endless. They would vote on a target and then we would set a plan in motion to steal said target from their lives, wipe their memory and begin to rebuild them in any way we wanted. Or they requested. Convince them of anything, or play with them like a lion would a mouse.

Each elite member could pay to have acts or stories performed. They would all have live feeds to all cameras where their prize would be held. If they paid enough they could even be involved in the act.

I smirked and tipped the whiskey placed in front of me by an attractive waitress who batted her eyelashes at every man at our table. The warmth coated my throat.

Hunter tapped his knee while everyone but Davies looked at him to continue. Hunter was the expert in this area and my go to person when I had business with other sex traffickers.

Davies had a leer on his face, he was convinced this wouldn't work and wasn't shy about making that known to his father, who was the only reason I allowed Davies to even be in on this meeting. "We want to see a trial run. Proof you can do as you claim. No disrespect, Troy! But this isn't your field of expertise. I have a friend, Daniel, who may be of some assistance in this area."

Hunter stiffened at the name and glowered at Davies. "You may not mean any disrespect but you forget he has me as his partner and even though I have every faith Troy is capable, we both know I am capable of breaking down a woman, or man, and you've tasted the proof, Davies. You forget your fucking place!"

My fist clenched under the table. I hated this cunt and although Hunter meant to take up for me, he made me look weak by coming to my defense.

"Holy shit, look at that." All heads spun to look in the direction his eyes were fixed on. My breath left me. Star. As beautiful as I remembered. Her hair was thick and hung in layers down her back, her trim physique that was toned in the right places made my dick awaken.

"Oh yeah, I forgot she comes here when in town." That little prick. "I'd pay anything to watch her though a live feed." He grunted. "Wasn't she the one who screwed you over?"

The table had grown eerily silent as my temper simmered on the edge of boiling over. How the hell did he know about her?

All eyes went to me as I stood and walked towards her. It was her. In the flesh. Her scent engulfed me. I dragged in some air to prepare myself. Grabbing her arm, I spun her to face me. She hadn't changed. The girl I fell in love with the girl who hardened my heart to impenetrable rock stared back at me. She was so close I could taste the breath that left her in a gasp. Her mouth dropped open, then smiled, then dropped back open. Her huge wide eyes formed tears, making her striking green irises glisten as she stared at me.

My hand slid down her arm to her hand. I shook when my finger brushed over a diamond on her ring finger. My eyes trailed the path my hand took and fell to her engagement ring. She snatched her hand back, drawing my eyes back to hers.

"Is it him?" I growled.

Her eyes squinted and her chest stuttered with her short, sharp breaths. "Dante?...

"Is it him?"

"You abandoned me," she whispered. To hear her soft voice again caused my heart to clench, but fury pushed it back as the image of when I had last seen her came tumbling back in, solidifying the ice once more.

"Because you're a whore!" I spat.

She inhaled, her eyes blinking and releasing the tears that had pooled in them. Her hand reared back and connected with my cheek before I could react or stop it.

She stormed from the restaurant, her chin as high as her defenses.

You could have heard a pin drop. Everyone had ceased eating; hell they'd even ceased breathing.

Turning back to our table, ten angry, judgmental eyes seared me. I let a woman, *that fucking woman,* humiliate me, making me look weak in their eyes. They saw women as objects beneath them.

I waltzed towards them, emanating confidence and power, and sat. Raising my glass, I lifted it in the air and grinned. "A toast. We have our trial run target gentlemen." I smirked.

Hunter had used his contacts to gather every single detail about the life of Faye Avery, Hollywood Queen, from birth up to the day in the restaurant. It was incredible that he had got every single detail, even her confidential medical records.

It was those I was reading through when my heart stopped. Flicking over the form, my eyes scanning but only registering certain parts.

Name - Faye Avery
Age – Seventeen
Known allergies – Penicillin

Termination – One foetus
Gestation - Eight weeks, three days
Method – Mifepristone

I couldn't breathe, my eyes blurring from staring at the same fact over and over

Seventeen! She was with me then. Did she kill my baby?

A month later, Hunter found a weakness in her staff. The assistant, Theo. Money hungry and power hungry. He would set up a trip for her and we would step in and take her. We would make her disappear, and I knew what method we would use. A plane crash. Poetic.

It had been so easy. Theo drugged her drink with a sleeping pill on the private plane he claimed to have hired for her. The plan went off without a hitch. The plane landed on private property, we torched it and we took her away. Once I had her in my arms she awoke from her slumber, her face pinching in confusion. My palm wrapped around her throat. "The baby you killed, was it mine?" Her eyes expanded to huge round orbs. "Answer me," I growled, tightening my hold.

Tears welled and dropped from her eyes as she whispered though the strain. "Yes."

That was all I needed. I injected her with more sedative and planned her demise.

Present

Everything was coming to a head, I could feel the end game approaching. I had stopped slipping the drug into her food over two weeks ago. Her memories would filter back in slowly but soon the truth would come crashing into her. I still loved her. I always would and I refused to let her go. This was their punishment for betraying me.

She stole my chance of becoming a father, all for what? So she could fuck around and still keep me on her leash and have both?

It wasn't something I had ever thought about, being a parent, but I wasn't given a choice. She killed something I put inside her, something created through the love I had for her then.

I would make her rectify everything she stole. He would feel the pain I felt.

I watched her run through the house and out the front door. Switching to the outdoor cameras, my heart flickered in my chest at her race towards the dock, her dainty hand holding over her heart.

She didn't know I had come home or that I had cameras in all the bathrooms of the house. So when she watched the pregnancy stick turn positive and spoke the words, "I'm pregnant," I heard and saw everything.

The end game had worked to perfection.

I stood when I saw a boat approach with a man holding up a huge camera.

CHAPTER 32

THE TRUTH

Star

I WAS SO IN MY own head I didn't hear the boat or the shouting until a flashing camera was in my face.

"Faye! Faye! Can you tell us why you let the world believe you died when your plane went down?"

What? The person barking stupid questions at me shoved a paper into my hands.

> The Hollywood Queen, world famous and adored starlet, Faye Avery is believed to have perished when her plane went down over a vineyard in Cyprus. The plane incinerated on impact.

I couldn't read anymore. It was like being hit with a tidal wave that destroyed the wall that was put up to hide my memories. Everything came flooding back into me. My lungs squeaked when the visions ploughed into my brain. It was like someone had clicked their fingers and my life hit me with the force of a train wreck. My knees buckled as my legs gave way and I fell to the floor, everything suddenly making perfect sense… perfect horrifying sense.

I was aware of Malik man-handling the guy asking questions as a fury found me and I pushed myself back upright, adrenaline forcing strength to overpower my weakened body.

"We were tipped off by a local who delivers mail here via speed-boat." The guy was answering Malik's questioning but my feet started moving, one in front of the other, until I stood in front of Dante who was blocking the entrance to our… no not our, HIS house.

"Why Dante?" I choked out. "Oh God, why did you do this to me?"

His face was stoic like he wasn't human. How could he do this to me? I loved him. When we were younger I thought he was my soul mate and would have given him anything. I aborted my child so he wouldn't find out and ruin his future. He would have stayed and dropped out of college to work a shit job so he could support me and I couldn't do that to him. Dante's were rare in this world and I recognized his greatness.

"I saw you!" My head tipped up to his, his angry eyes holding my confused ones. "I didn't leave. I came to your house and saw you leave with him. You went to a motel and stayed in there all night with him. How long were you fucking him behind my back?"

What? Oh my God.

My head shook as I answered him, completely defeated. "I had to take these pills," I said. "They force an abortion to happen. You get really sick and I needed someone with me. I couldn't do it at my house; you know what my mom was like." *Is like.* She wasn't dead. He had lied about that too.

He looked pale.

"I would never cheat on anyone Dante, and God, I loved you so fiercely. I died the day they told me your plane went down. I was never the same and when we got news you were never on the plane, I have never felt more joy in my life but then the fact you didn't contact me broke me all over again. I was clueless to why you abandoned me. I thought you liked your new life and had maybe met someone else."

A choked sob ripped from me as tears cascaded down my face,

their torrent tearing my soul out of my body with them. "Do you know what that does to a soul that's so in love and attached to another? To endure pain like that was truly unbearable. No one could drag me from the depression. Then months passed, a year, and I relearnt how to be me again. To breathe for me, to wake up and know I was alone and I needed to keep living."

"But you're with him!" he screamed at me, making me flinch and step back.

"Three years later, Dante!" I screamed back and hammered my fists at his chest. "What have you done? What did you turn me into?"

My sobs turned to frantic wails when the reality of everything I had become settled in my chest. I had betrayed my real fiancé, the man I was crazy about. He had saved me and reassembled the damaged shadow of the girl that was left after Dante. He rebuilt me piece by piece, by letting me heal myself, by showing me I was worthy of living a good life, and that I had something to offer the world. That I was still loved and still valued and needed. Now I was disgusting and ruined. He would never forgive me for becoming what I was now.

My legs gave out, my body colliding with a crash on the concrete beneath me. How could Dante turn into this? He was sick, cruel to an unimaginable degree. He kidnapped me, he manipulated me, lied, betrayed…ruined me. How did he get away with this?

Dante's shadow fell over me. "You belong to me."

A hysterical laugh bubbled up and ripped from my lips. "I belong to him and I will go to him." Even if he turned me away, I still needed to go to him. He was where I belonged.

Anger coated me in its venom as it dripped from Dante's demeanor. "You belong to me and you are staying here through choice!"

My eyes sprung to his. Was he insane?

"You will tell him and everyone else you have been away on a secret getaway to marry your lover. You had no idea of the media storm."

He was certifiable. Freaking crazy son of a bitch!

"Screw you!" I spat.

He dropped on his haunches, gripping my jaw with his fingers, and lifted my face to his. "I have everything on tape, Star."

My stomach vaulted, threatening to expel the contents.

"You begging me to fuck you in the cell. Every depraved act inside the house. Your pleasure from all the dirty things you let me, hell, begged me to do to you. Malik watching… seeing your pussy on full view."

The bile burned my throat. The tears blinded my vision. The frantic pound of my blood made me lightheaded.

"I'll leak everything first to him, and then to the media."

"Why do you hate me?" I sobbed. I was dizzy and on the verge of passing out. The torrent of memories, the truth of everything was too overwhelming, and the loss and ache from what I knew I could never have back was unbearable.

"We will go through with the wedding and then you'll give me the child you should have given me years ago."

My breath left me, along with a long high-pitched sound. I was pregnant. Did he know? Did he plan that?

"I have cameras everywhere, Star… even in the toilets."

Star… that had been his pet name for me. No one called me Star any more.

I was drowning in despair, my heart bleeding… crying for its mate… Cade.

Cade

Faye. God, she was there again in my dreams, so vivid I could smell her scent. "Argh!" I screamed, smothering my face in her pillow, the one I traveled with. I didn't give a fuck if that made me a pussy. Yeah, I was a film star but I was also human and I was dying inside without her.

My body wept in sorrow, my heart beat out of my chest. I wanted this crippling throb to ease so I could focus on anything but the hole in the pit of my stomach that swallowed another piece of me every day I woke up without her. I wanted to be set free from the ache that was constant since the day they told me her plane went down.

I loved her then and my love for her now was killing me slowly.

Men are funny creatures. We love fiercely when we find the right woman. Family, friends… none of it matters when you have the one. We fly the nest and our love and life, our everything, revolves around the love we harbor for our woman. Don't get me wrong, I loved my family, friends but if it came down to a choice, she would have won every time.

I didn't need anyone but her. Men don't need much to function, it's true what they say; you only need the love of a good woman. I had that and lost it.

I couldn't believe she was gone. If she was dead, I would have felt it, I would have ceased to exist. I was barely existing now; an apparition of my former self. I was only breathing for the sake of living but not really present in the world. My heart was dying; there was still a beat but there was no sound.

Thoughts tore at my mind. Was she scared? The sound of the impact, the twisting and crunching of metal, the whooshing of air as it was sucked from the cabin. The heat from the fire that lit up the engine on impact. My beautiful girl, scared, screaming and crying. Did she think about me as fear took hold of her and held her in its grip?

They found no bodies. They said the fire was too bad and refused to allow us the pictures. I knew my woman was still out there. My soul was tethered to hers and it still sensed her essence. I would find her. I would never rest until I found her.

My phone buzzed, startling me. I reached across the bed and grabbed my cell. My best friend Jenson had finally text.

I have someone willing to take us to the location of the crash site. Be ready in one hour

At last, progress. I would start there.

An hour later I waited outside my hotel room for Jenson. I pulled my baseball cap down further over my sunglasses and tightened the hoody so my lips and nose were barely on show. I looked like a weirdo but that meant people stayed away. I couldn't risk being recognized by a fan.

I ignored the heat as it soaked into the black fibers and made sweat pool in every pore. I sighed in relief when Jenson pulled up in a van, until he gestured for me to get in the back. My brow scrunched but I was too anxious to bother arguing. I opened the back and got in.

A scrawny guy sat in the back looking like someone was about to jump out and shank him. He was nervous, his eyes moving rapidly in his head, his teeth worrying his bottom lip.

I shut the door and ignored the guy itching at his arm like something was crawling under his skin. I was in the film industry and my best friend Jenson was a famous rock star. I knew a tweaker when I was shut in a van with one.

"Please tell me you're not our tour guide?"

He looked up at me, then away, shaking his head. "No tour needed, sir." Sir? I didn't think anyone had ever called me *sir* before. I waved my hand in a continue gesture. I was being irritated at breakneck speed. "I work out in the field where this plane crash happened. It's a vineyard. I pick grapes, sir. We were told not to come into work that day but I left something there the day before and I needed it, so I crept in." His eyes kept darting to the door like he was waiting for it to fly open. What the hell was he scared of? His hand went back to tearing into his flesh. "A plane landed right out in the field, it was amazing. I have never seen a plane up close before."

My heart was on a rampage, raging war with my ribcage. "When you say landed, you mean crashed?"

He stared straight at me, his eyes finding focus as he leaned forward. "There was no crash, sir. The plane landed perfectly and a car came. Men went on board and came out with a woman. She was unconscious and then they placed her in the car."

My woman, my fiancée, the love of my life was alive… but taken, which meant she could be found and whoever had stolen what was mine would die painfully, choking on his own blood.

I couldn't breathe. The anger, fear and relief all bombarded me at once. There was no air. My phone vibrated against my leg grounding me. Slipping it free the number was unknown.

"Who's this?"

I heard a gasp then a drop of the phone. Then … her!

"I'm sorry. I'm going to get ready now."

I scrambled to loosen the hood, pulling off my hat and glasses, trying to suck in oxygen. My Faye …

"Faye… Faye..."

The line was dead.

The tweaker's audible gasp brought me back. God, of course he would recognize me, fucking figures. Why was he scrambling for the door? Usually they scrambled towards me.

Turning to me, his head shook from side to side as his wide eyes filled with fear and confusion. "You were there. Is this a test? Please don't kill me."

Shit, he was tripping out on something; a bad batch of whatever he pumped into those veins. He was so pale, you'd have thought the devil had appeared to him.

"Dude, relax, you're about to stroke out." I tried moving towards him but he flinched and started crying. I banged on the adjoining wall to get Jenson's attention.

I heard his door open and close before the back of the van opened. The tweaker spilled free, landing in a heap at Jenson's feet. "It is him! He killed Rahul and stole the woman!" he yammered at Jenson in a panic.

It took five seconds for it to register. A further two for me to collapse to my knees. And one more before his name left my lips in disbelief. My brother… my twin brother… "Dante!"

y
Continue their story in book 2… CADENCE ← Don't grumble we warned you!

Keep reading for a sneak peek at other work and upcoming releases

CADENCE

Cade.

He had her love. Her devotion. He destroyed her with it!

Years I loved Faye Avery from a distance, watched my brother have something he didn't deserve. She was always too good for him. Dante had a need for control and that grew with him from childhood, infecting her to bend to his whim.

When Dante abandoned her, the girl who put his future and needs before her own, I rediscovered the girl who lost herself to the heartache. She blossomed and flourished in the light of the love she deserved - until he robbed me of her. Breaking her down, dimming the essence of the woman she had become.

Dante had a darkness inside him that led him down a path of depravity. He was too far gone. He functioned on corruption, humiliation, power and retribution, and all for something that never happened.

What he forgets is this! I not only wear his face, I carry the darkness inside of me too, and my wrath will coat him with it so thick he will drown under the rain of my reckoning.

He wants Star, a memory of a girl he used to know. He stole Faye, a woman who owns my heart and is the cadence in mine.

I will find him.

I will find him. I will take her from him.

And then I will kill him.

Out now

empathy

by KER DUKEY

Preface

Blake

My birth name is Damian. Fitting, really, or so I'm told by the woman who named me.

"You're the devil's son," she would spit at me, pointing a shaky finger in my cheek in a drug induced haze whenever I refused to bend to her whim. I can still feel the impression of her fingertip where her nail broke the skin. I go by Blake now; it's my middle name, chosen by the midwife who brought me back from the dead. My mother couldn't wait for me to be out of her womb, expelling me too early from her body with the cord wrapped neatly around my neck, almost robbing me of the life I'd been gifted by a drunken fondle in the back of a truck.

They say some people are born with decreased activity in the brain; a cold spot in the front central lobe. Where most people have activity, a hot area giving them feelings, emotions and enabling them to love, there are a rare few who have a cold spot, affecting their ability to feel emotions, *empathy*. There are theories that serial killers have this cold spot. Psychopaths. That's why they lack the ability to connect, to care.

I don't have feelings the way most people do. I may be one of those people/psychopaths. I don't know. What I do know is I can fuck the woman who claims to love me and leave her before the sweat's even dried on my skin, knowing she will cry herself to sleep. I can supply my mother with cash to fund her drug habit, hoping this will be the final hit to send her to the afterlife *and*... I can kill without remorse.

My emotions are corrupted, have been since my life changed in a single night. My ability to give a shit is absent. I don't care about anyone with the exception of my kid brother, who is the sole reason I became a killer to begin with. Maybe I would have killed no matter what. Some people are born predestined to become evil, to mark the world with their darkness. Some paint the world in techno color, I paint it in red; blood red.

Can circumstances change us? Can the evil doings of others force us to change the path we're on? To alter the warmth in our souls? Can they dim our light, making us cold, dark, evil? I don't know. I've questioned this before, but now I accept this is who I am. Just like we cannot choose when the sun will rise and when it will set, I could not choose my destiny. It was mapped out for me. When life drowns you in its cruelty, you don't know which way the current will drag you, or who you'll be once you re-surface.

What I do know is, my emotions switched off when I came home from a party at eighteen years old, fully expecting a beat down by my Step father for coming home drunk after telling him I wouldn't be home that night. Instead I found him in my eleven-year-old brother's bed. I literally felt myself change. A flick of a switch. If there ever was a warm spot, it turned cold in that moment with the rest of me. Reasoning became impossible, questions I never thought I would have to ask raped my once placid mind. Shutters came down inside me, closing over the windows to my soul, changing me forever.

The muffled cries of my brother, muted because his head was pushed into his pillow while his own flesh and blood, the man who created him, the man supposed to protect, love and cherish him was naked above him, changed my direction in life; mine and Ryan's, creating my step father's fate in the process.

I didn't even flinch when I walked up silently behind him. The drunken haze cleared, nothing but rage burned in my veins, a blood red fog clouding my vision. Rage wasn't an emotion in that moment, it was an entity grown from the darkest depths of my being, vibrating through my skin to be released. Nothing felt more right than allowing it to take control, seek retribution for the abuse we were born into, to let it consume the boy who once lived there, devouring any human part left of my soul.

The darkness I harbored deep inside that we all have under the surface took control. I gripped his head, and with all the strength I had, I twisted until I heard the loud pop, click, snap, whatever you want to call the sound of his neck breaking, ending his life and shutting off his switch to the stained soul inside him.

I dragged his warm, sweaty body away from my brother, out of his room, closing the door behind me. Alcohol and sweat seeped from his pores, assaulting my nose and making my stomach twist with more hate than I knew possible. I dropped him at the top of the stairs and nudged him with my foot. His lifeless body thumped down, landing in a heap at the bottom. The man who gave my brother life, who had been all I knew as a father figure was now nothing but a decomposing body. If I could have killed him again and again, I would have, without hesitation. I went to the shower and turned it on before going back to my brother's room and scooping up his trembling body. I put him on his feet, told him to shower and promised no one would ever hurt him again.

When I called the police the next morning, telling them I got up to find my dad had an accident, they didn't question my story that he was a drunk, and no one cared enough to argue foul play. The reports said accidental death. Our father was well known for liking the bottle.

Ryan and I moved in with our waste-of-life mother, and if it wouldn't have been suspicious for both our parents to have accidents in such a small time frame, I would have killed her too. Instead, I gave her money to disappear for days at a time until I turned twenty-two, finished my degree in criminal justice, joined the police force and got custody of Ryan. Then I paid her to disappear to distant relatives.

I took martial arts classes and shooting lessons after that night. I wanted to be able to protect my brother from any threat. I earned extra money through my computer skills to buy Ryan anything he needed and to support our mother's habit. Ever since I was little I knew computers. I can hack pretty much any network, and I used that skill to earn petty cash from students wanting grades changed, or finding information on people that was kept in confidential files. I worked solely through my computer; I couldn't risk my identity being compromised. To contact me you had to already know about me through word of mouth, then email one of my many accounts that would go into spam file I never opened, so if someone stumbled across that email account, it looked inactive on my part.

This system also worked for me when I became a contract killer. I can see the sender's email address without having to open the email. Just having that small piece of information, I can get into their emails, send viruses that clone their hard drives, giving me access to everything they do, which in turn gives me passwords to their accounts, including their online banking. I can find out every single thing about them and their life with one simple address, and if I find them trustworthy and wealthy enough to afford me, I bring up a chat box, scaring the shit out of them. I have two more chats with them before completing the job they want me for. Then I never speak to them again.

I have only a few rules:

One: Never do more than one job per client. Once they see how easy it is to get away with murder they tend to become a little kill happy. They would have me killing the neighbor for playing music too loud if they could.

Two: Never take a job close to home. When people use the term 'don't shit where you eat' well, I don't kill where I live. It just makes sense.

Three: No one knows who I am, my name, age, what I look like or if I'm even male; which is why everything is done through an untraceable computer.

I make a shit load for my services. I have to be clever not to flash my cash, swapping my funds into offshore accounts and getting a normal job so I look like everyone else. That's why I joined the police force; who better to teach you how to kill and how to avoid being caught than the police?

My life course was chosen that night when I was eighteen, when I took a life and didn't feel remorse. When I overheard some rich college kid telling his friend he would pay a million for someone to kill his overbearing father, I knew he was talking hypothetically but I also knew there were people who would pay for someone to kill for them and right then, in that moment, my career path was chosen. It took me six months in the academy, training, three months field training, two years cut loose on patrol and I made detective at the tender age of twenty-five. I'm the youngest detective to ever be sworn in at our department but I'm good at my job. Just like they train me to be a better killer, who better to find criminals then a master criminal?

THE BROKEN

BY

KER DUKEY

PROLOGUE
River

It's the night of my sixteenth birthday, sweet sixteen. Everyone's sixteenth should be memorable. Mine will be, just not for the right reasons.

Sammy's hands are touching my skin, his breath on my neck, and his words in my ear. He's my brother's best friend, and our next door neighbour. He's the same age as my brother, two years older than me, and he has always been my first and only crush. I've felt things for him since the first day I laid eyes on his dark, unruly hair and soul-warming blue eyes. His smile is sweet; his laugh gives me goose bumps. His eyes light up whenever I enter a room and I know he feels the same way about me. He used to call me Twinkle Toes because I'm a dancer, and as I got older, Twinkle Toes became just Twink. He's who I feel inside me, taking my virginity. He's loving me, caressing my skin, giving me that special first time all girls should have. He looks into my eyes, tells me how beautiful I am, how much he loves me. He is who I feel sliding his length in and out of my sacred place.

"I love you so much, you know that right? You owe me this, River."

His words break through my daydream, Sammy's image fades, and Danny's takes its place. His tears drip into my neck, itching my skin; his fingers slightly pinching the skin on my cheek as he holds my face to one side. His heavy body weights me down, pinning me to my small childhood twin bed. A burning sensation and a sharp stabbing pain assaults me as he thrusts inside me. I hold back my screams, swallow them down, burying them, but I'm worried if I hold the tears in they will flow inside me, drowning me, and so I let them flow from my eyes. My pillow soaks them into its soft plump fibre; the pillow that usually offers me comfort at night will now forever hold the tears from my stolen innocence. He thrusts harder and grunts before his body relaxes and I feel more of his weight press against my small frame, making it hard for me to breath. He's still muddy from the garden; it's dirtied my sheets and nighty. He grips my chin and forces me to look into his dark brown eyes. "You belong to me. What I did for you and your brother, I'll never tell anyone if you admit you belong to me and that you wanted this."

I force down the lump in my throat and ask him why he's crying. His eyes narrow. "Because I love you and you just gave me something beautiful, now say you belong to me." He growls the last words, his grip tightening on my chin. "I…I…belong …to...y…you," I stutter.

He grins and lifts from my body. There's a burning ache between my thighs. I wait for my door to close behind him as he leaves before I pull my knees up to my chest and roll into the fetus position. I cry, broken. I cry for my brother, I cry for my father, I cry for my stolen innocence, and I cry for Sammy. I was meant for him.

Out now!

KER DUKEY'S LINKS

Website – www.kerdukey.com/
Facebook - https://www.facebook.com/KerDukeyauthor
Twitter - https://twitter.com/KerDukeyauthor
Amazon page - http://www.amazon.com/Ker-Dukey/e/B00H7B3VEM/
ref=sr_ntt_srch_lnk_1?qid=1410003592&sr=1-1
Newsletter - http://kerdukey.us8.list-manage.com/subscribe?u=5af0eb-
98c37e6fb4193f03c1a&id=14c71ad5c7

Other titles by Ker Dukey

The Broken
The Broken Parts Of Us
My Soul Keeper
The Beats In Rift
Empathy

The Decimation of Mae

Book 1 in the Blue Butterfly Series

D H Sidebottom

Prologue

The Devil visited me three times in my life; albeit, my short life. Not in the physical sense, you must understand, but very much literally.

He was persistent, resolute and tenacious. His ruthless greed to annihilate me was utterly disturbing. I am sure if he had hierarchy, the man at the top would have dragged his arse into Hell's prison for his unscrupulous methods.

I was just fifteen when I first became aware of what he was capable of. This initial taste of him set the playing field for how my life was to be *lived* – for want of a better word.

He mocked me, showed me mercilessly how he played the game and how he liked to cheat at said game. He ridiculed and taunted me until, six months later, he won and took something of so much importance from me that I would never be the same again.

His second visit was, in my eyes, so much more cruel and heartless. I know we're talking about the Devil here, and yes, you have a right to say he had no heart but even then, even when I was so utterly broken, I begged to differ and hoped – no, prayed – that somewhere deep in the caverns of his black, tortured soul there was something that beat and confused his emotions once in a while.

The third visit was somewhat different than the other two. He tried, and at first succeeded to bring me to my knees once and for all, but then something happened. God finally intervened and altered Satan's intention; he sent hope and morphed the Devil's minion into an Angel, hoping to break and shatter the anguish and suffering. He gave the ability for me to feel pleasure in pain, order in the chaos and light in the darkness.

But in giving me a reprieve, he also gave me something that would finally and ultimately obliterate me. He gave me the capability to love, therefore giving me the ability to be destroyed.

And Satan made sure that I *was* destroyed. Cruelly, viciously and sadistically.

I am Mae Swift, and this is the story of my decimation.

by D H Sidebottom

Olivia Thomas is in love, pure, simple soul consuming love. Nathan Carter is her other half, her light, her passion.

After three years of being together at university; three years of being joined, of a love so intense, passionate and spirited they thought their future was safe and endless but life always finds a cruel way to interfere and they soon find their relationship can't withstand destiny's intrusions and obstacles.

Two decades later destiny apologises and brings them back together by sheer chance, re-igniting their intense passion, connection and love but they soon find that twenty years of life, secrets and lies creates difficulties and struggles even their bond might struggle to endure.

When an evil from Olivia's past returns to haunt them and rip apart everything they have managed to build back up, can the lovers survive with their love and souls still intact…or their lives?

D H Sidebottom's Links

Website: http://dhsidebottom.co.uk
FB page: https://www.facebook.com/DHSidebottom
Twitter: https://twitter.com/DHSidebottom
Amazon: http://www.amazon.co.uk/D-H-Sidebottom/e/B00C3ELG1I/
ref=sr_ntt_srch_lnk_2?qid=1410603361&sr=1-2

Dawn's Acknowledgments

Okay, here comes the soppy bit!

We always start with the word 'Thanks' at this bit – such a simple word, but never used enough. Yet sometimes, it isn't enough either.

'Thanks' doesn't seem the appropriate word for my gratitude to my children and my Mum. 'Thanks' isn't appreciation enough for their relentless support, belief and encouragement. 'Thanks' is nowhere near adequate for the days when they feed me when I forget to eat, tackle the huge ironing pile I overlook, or when they shop to sustain my caffeine addiction when I am too engrossed in a book to visit the store. Or even the way they each take care of me, as well as each other on the days when the words swallow me.

There isn't a word, or even a phrase, out there that can define what I want to say to them, apart from, I love you, because as simple as it is, it says everything.

And yet again, here comes that inadequate word; Thanks. But this time it is to the five special friends in my life. Vickie, Michelle, Debbie, Kelly and Nikki. When the darkness threatens to devour me, you are each there, flicking on the light that chases the shadows away. You make me laugh when I cry, you give me hope through all the impossibility and you hold me up when all I want to do is fall, but more than that, you protect me from my own demons – you keep me breathing! I love each one of you.

And finally, to a very special woman. Miss Ker Dukey. I know you will cringe and hate me for saying this, but you're my guardian Angel, my best friend, my soul sister, and my sanity. Not a day goes by when you don't make me smile.

This career can bring the most gruelling stress, the utmost heartache and the greatest agony, but for all those difficulties, there are infinite valuable rewards. And the most treasured of those is that it brought us together, not just as writers but as friends.

But above all, I want to thank you for having enough faith in me to allow me to write alongside your amazing talent.

And one day, when we are rich enough to retire to the Bahamas with our families, I will kiss your sweaty, but damn sexy, feet.

Luv ya' babe ♡

Ker's Acknowledgments

As always thank you to my family... who lose me every time a character demands their story be written. I love you and appreciate all you do.

Thank you to Dawn for entertaining me when I asked, "you want to write this book with me? A woman wakes up with no memory and..." ← And that was it, she cut me off and said, "Hell yes!" Boom! A couple of funny phone calls to outline the story, a couple of months of back forth and endless messages of ideas and FaCade was born.

Dawn you have been so easy and a pleasure to work with, your talent is endless. You are the twist in my spiral, the dark in my black, the crazy in my insanity and the kink in my depravity. I freaking love you.

Thanks to our amazing Kittens and hardcore fans who pimp us all the time! You get us out there and we love you. My girl Crystal who loves me. My girls Kiki and Judi who are not only my publicists but friends who I adore even when Judi's sexy hubby makes me blush ;)

To all the blogs who review, pimp and promo us. Thank you!!

A special thanks to Kirsty Moseley for guest reading beta ARC. You rock lady!

Thank you to the people who make it all happen.

Authors- D.H Sidebottom & Ker Dukey
Beta's – Vickie Leaf, Vikki Ryan, Kelly Graham, Jillian Crouson–
Toth, Terrie Arasin, Katie Theobald, Michelle McGinty.
Editor – Kyra Lennon
http://www.kyralennon.com/
Proof read – Jillian Crouson
Cover model - Justin Marcoccio
https://www.facebook.com/Justin.Marcoccio.info
Photographer – Christopher John
https://www.facebook.com/CJCPhotography
Promo - Concierge Literary Promotions
Website – http://www.clpromotionsky.net/#!about/c24vq
Facebook page - www.facebook.com/CLPromotionsKY
Formatting – Champagne Formats

Printed in Great Britain
by Amazon

36559258R00116